THE TARGET H

THE PENETRATOR 1

CHET CUNNINGHAM

WOLFPACK
PUBLISHING
— EST 2013 —

The Penetrator: The Target "H"
Chet Cunningham

Paperback Edition

Wolfpack Publishing
6032 Wheat Penny Avenue
Las Vegas, NV 89122

ISBN: 978-1-64119-863-9

DEDICATION

To the two Andys—a couple of winners—for all the help they have given Mark Hardin.
And to Mick and all the others who have fought the Silent War...it was not in vain.

THE TARGET H

BIOGRAPHICAL PROFILE

SUBJECT: HARDIN, MARK ALLEN
LAST KNOWN ADDRESS: P.O. Box 86, Barstow, Calif.
RESIDENCE: Calico Mountains

PHYSICAL DATA:

Age: 28
DOB/Place: 20 Aug. '45, Los Angeles, Calif. (Queen of Angels Hospital)
Height: 6' 2"
Weight: 174
Eyes: Brown/Black
Hair: Black, straight
Complexion: Clear/Olive
Race: Cauc. & American
Religion: Does not practice.
Hat Size: 11A
Shoes: 10 EE
Waist: 31" Inseam: 34" Chest: 48" (barrel chested)
Sleeve: 33" Shoulders: 46" Neck: 16"
Glove Size: #9 (medium)
Marks or Scars: 1) Bullet wound, 7cm below left

elbow. Bullet wound(s) (estimated from automatic weapon fire), 3cm below right hip joint, 11cm below same, 19cm below same, 2) Shrapnel wound 3) Scar tissue along right and left occipital ridge (result of boxing injuries) 4) Sickle-shaped scar, extending from point of left scapula, under left arm, to point 2cm left of sternum (result of childhood accident) [L.A. County General Hospital report indicates injury result of auto accident at age of four, when parents and three siblings killed.]

<u>Operations</u>

Internal Injuries:

1) Dislocation of right shoulder, right hip, severe trauma to muscles of sacro-lumbar region (result of severe beating sustained in Saigon, Republic of Viet-nam, 31 Aug. -1 Sept. 72) 2) Compressed disc(s), sacro-lumbar region (result of football injury while playing for UGJLA in 1966 (Rose Bowl Game).

3) Broken right ulna, fully healed (result of fall from tree at age ten.

4) T&A at age six.

Education: Graduate, San Fernando High School, June, 1962. Graduate, A.B., UCLA, June, 1966.

Major Subject: Languages (German, Spanish)

Minor Subject: Police Science. Athletic Record: 1) NRA Junior Rifle Competition, fired in regional matches; 1956, 443; 1957, 461; 1958, 489.

2) AAU Golden Gloves (Middle weight) Jr. Division. 1958-6 w, 3 ls; 1959-7 w, 2 ls; 1960-9 w, 01s.

3) San Fernando High-Lettered in: Track: I960, 1961,1962. Football: Same.

4) UCLA-Lettered in: Track: 1963, 1964,1965 (Football injury, 1 Jan. '66, prevented participation in Track events in 1966) Football: 1962, '63, '64, '65. Wrestling: 1964, 1965.

Boxing: 1963, 1964.

MILITARY RECORD:

Volunteer enlistment, U.S. Army, 27 Dec. 1966.

ASN: RA 59 637 242

Highest Rank Attained: M/Sgt., E-7

Discharged: Honorable, 26 Dec. '72.

Area 1 Score (AGCT): 136 (possible 140)

Basic Training: Fort Ord, California, 3 Jan. - 3 Mar. '67.

Advance Infantry Training: Fort Benning, GA., 20 Mar. - 21 May '67.

MOS Training (Primary): Army Language School, Monterey, Calif., 25 May - 24 Sept. '67.

ARDEF Language Proficiency:

1) German 2) Spanish 3) Vietnamese Advanced

2) MOS Tng.: Army Intelligence School, Ft. Meade, MD, 10 Oct.'67 - 9 Jan.'68.

Assigned: Presidio, San Francisco, CA, 10 Feb. '68.

Assigned: Headquarters, I Corps, G-2, Quang Doc, Repub. Vietnam, 4 April 1969.

Reassigned: Presidio, San Francisco, CA, 11 Oct. 70.
Assigned: Headquarters, 3d Army, Saigon, Repub. Vietnam, 118th C.I.C. Det. 21 Nov. '71.
Transferred: U.S. Army Hospital, San Francisco, CA 3 Sept. 72.
Discharged: HONORABLE. 26 Dec. '72.
Decorations and Awards: Silver Star; 12 Aug. '69.
(without citations Bronze Star; 5 May 70.
listed here) Oak Leaf; 11 May '70. Purple Heart; 12 Aug. '69. Oak Leaf; 6 May '70. 2nd Oak Leaf; 3 Sept. 72.
(First citation) Good Conduct; 3 Feb. '67
Subject is qualified EXPERT in: M-14, M-16 rifle, .45 pistol, M-6 & A-3 light machine gun, M-79 grenade launcher, M-1921-A-1 .45 SMG (Thompson), 9mm Uzi SMG
Subject is qualified SHARPSHOOTER: AK-47 V (Chinese) Assault rifle, M-3 .45 SMG, M-38 Schmeisser SMG, M-42 Makarov rifle, M-51 Skoda SMG, U.S. 60 & 81mm mortars, 3.5 & 4" rocket launchers, 106mm recoilless rifle, .38 M&P revolver.
Subject is also considered EXPERT IN USE OF:
Hand grenades, explosives, booby traps, land mines and other hazardous devices.
Subject is also considered HIGHLY QUALIFIED in use of: knife, garrote, crossbow, toga sticks.
Subject is known to be a former AAU (Golden Gloves) boxer, holds 2d Dan (Black) Belt in Karate, 1st Dan (Black) Belt in Aikido.

POLICE RECORD: Subject is not known to have prior arrests or convictions of record.
NOTICE TO ALL LEO: Subject is to be considered armed and very dangerous. Approach with extreme caution.

PROLOGUE

CURLING GRAY TENDRILS OF FOG STILL WAFTED along the streets, turning the hills overlooking San Francisco Bay into a surrealistic painting come true. From time to time the soldier standing on the sidewalk would catch glimpses of the tops of the spans of the Bay Bridge, peeking in and out of the dense morning fog that covered the bay. He felt the chilly dampness intensely. It was very different from the moist heat of the tropics, and three months confinement in a hospital, with its controlled environment, had done nothing to prepare him.

He shrugged and glanced down at his belongings, brought outside by a helpful orderly. A metal-jacketed footlocker, stenciled with his name, rank, and serial number; a twill barracks bag; and the soldier's companion, his "AWOL" bag. Under one arm, he carried everything else he possessed, his discharge papers and a copy of his 201 jacket.

He felt a twinge of pain as he moved to peer down the street toward town...still no sign of a taxi. The long wait was typical of his recent bad luck. Pain caused an involuntary gasp to slip from his lips as he turned back to stare out over the fog-bound bay.

There was nothing more that could be done for him, the doctors had said. Skilled efforts had returned to him the use of his arm—it had been carefully slipped back into joint, and he had been given hours of therapy. His ribs were healing properly and about as fast as could be expected, the collarbone had knit with only a small lump, and—it was thought, but never expressed directly—the chances were that the nonspecific pain in his back was mostly psychosomatic. So many similar complaints from Vietnam returnees had proven to be so. Psychosomatic or not, the damn thing hurt constantly.

It was not a bomb blast or hidden land mine that had wrenched his body into this twisted agony. He had been viciously beaten—by fellow Americans stationed in Saigon—because he had been investigating thefts of government property and the black market.

Stolen government ammunition, food, booze, commodities of all sorts had been getting into civilian hands; drugs had been flowing in the other direction. Somehow his cover had been blown, and the beating came as a matter of course. He had been left for dead, which he nearly was, and not thought of again by those whose lucrative racket he had exposed.

At least he was not thought of until it was learned that he had survived and was talking his head off. The tentacles of the black market racket extended even here, to the hallways of Letterman General Hospital. He had been attacked twice, silently and viciously, while undergoing corrective therapy for his dislocated shoulder. Both attacks were interrupted before they could become fatal, but they had interfered with his recovery. The pain in his back, he knew, was a recurrence of a preservice injury. For that reason, they had declared that it was not a service-connected disability. But no matter how many doctors wagged their heads and talked to him about his mental state, he was convinced that the beating had done irreparable damage to his back—that he was doomed to remain a cripple for life.

Lights cut through the fog, and a taxi pulled to the curb. The driver did not climb out of his hack; he spoke through a rolled-down window.

"Where to, bub?"

"International Airport, please," replied the soldier.

"Right." The driver sat fast.

"Uh, say, would you mind giving me a hand with this stuff?"

A look of scorn crossed the driver's face. What the hell, this guy was bigger than him, over six feet, big shoulders and chest, maybe close to two hundred pounds. All those white teeth in a dark, tough face like that. And he expects a servant. The cabbie dragged himself out of his vehicle and opened the trunk. The footlocker looked heavy and the union rules forbade him to pick up anything over fifty pounds. Master Sergeant, he saw from the stenciled information on the footlocker. Fuckin' NCOs. Always lookin' for someone to do their work. Then he remembered where he was picking up this fare: Letterman General Hospital. On closer inspection; he saw the white marks that showed recently healed cuts on the guy's face. He must have been busted up pretty bad. Quickly, secretly contrite for his previous thoughts, he loaded the gear.

As they sped along, the Cabbie tried to make up for his earlier mood. After all, the guy had all but screamed just gettin' into the cab. Must be all busted up inside. Why the hell they let them out so soon anyway? He began to jabber, trying to draw out his passenger. "You was in 'Nam, Buddy? Right?" He got no answer. "Ya'll have it pretty rough over there, Buddy?" Undaunted, he tried another tack. "Say, I know what it's like. I was in the Big One myself."

His passenger was not answering, because his passenger wasn't listening. His mind was going over and over the same thing he had been thinking for the past month. Busted up and busted out. Discharged from the hospital and discharged from the army in the same day.

DECEMBER 26, 1972. Happy fucking Holidays...

HE DIDN'T THINK of his future, because he didn't, believe he had one. Where does a guy go for a job when the least movement nearly makes him scream his head off? His discharge read Honorable, but with a medical rider declaring him unfit for continued service his military career was ended, totally, completely. And, if rumor could be believed, his war was nearly ended as well, only a pen stroke away from peace.

He had joined the army, filled with idealism and love of country and his fellow Americans. It gave him a sour, hopeless feeling to know that it was not an action of the enemy, wounds received honorably in battle, but the fists, clubs and brass knuckles of his own people, fellow Americans, that had ended his military career.

It might not be as bad as he thought, he had to admit to himself, boarding his flight to LA and getting settled in his seat. The muscles of his arms, shoulders and legs—rather than protesting—began to relax and function normally. As the plane leveled out over the Pacific, heading South, he found himself starting to think differently about his condition.

After all, he told himself, the bruises are gone, cuts healed—ribs and collarbone too. Maybe the doctors were right. Maybe it was just lack of practice: A sudden twinge partly deflated his newly acquired optimism. His damn back! Oh, sure, the compressed discs were there before he joined the army, but having someone jump up and down on the small of his back was no picnic.

Through it all, the months of confinement amid agony, the army had maintained that there was no new, visible damage—nothing to explain the pain he felt—and that left him out in the cold. For his own part, he was convinced that the new injuries were permanent.

The pronouncement by the shrinks that overcoming the disabling pain would have to be done by himself, neither angered him, nor increased his habitual bitterness. What the hell, he'd been on his own almost as long as he could remember. Living alone with his pain would be nothing new.

His gloomy thoughts diminished during lunch, served by a pert, big-breasted, mini-skirted stew. It pleased him to discover the ease with which he handled coping with variations of balance caused by the plane's motion through the air, and eating in a limited amount of space without leaving half his meal on his shirtfront. His spirits soared again. A natural optimism began to win out.

Growing up as a welfare kid—an orphan farmed out to one foster family after another—he repeatedly ran away and was returned to the Children's Home. It gave a boy a certain resilience, an ability to bounce back.

Then the right one came, the home that did work. It was the warm, laughing home of Sean Patrick Michael Doolin, a Sergeant in the Los Angeles Police Department. Here, he had learned to use Golden Gloves boxing matches to exercise his muscles and relieve his aggressions. He'd completed four years of high school while living with the family of the good-natured policeman, finishing near the top of his class and winning a scholarship to UCLA. It had been his athletic prowess, as much or more than his academic record, that had opened the high-priced doors of that prestigious university. Wrestling, football and track; he'd lettered in all three in high school and was considered a natural athlete. He was a sure thing to go pro.

His involvement with sports had led to the injury that complicated his present situation. He was a senior at UCLA, practicing for the UCLA-Michigan State Rose Bowl game. It was a big deal—for the schools, and for the players, students and gamblers. It was the first time in over ten years that UCLA had made it to the Rose Bowl. As the star running back, he had been approached by gambling interests and offered a lot of money to see that the game went the way they wanted it to go. Faithful to the code of ethics, he reported it to his coach. There was a quick, quiet round up of the gamblers and he forgot it until the final practice.

The team was rehearsing a simple line plunge play. He was carrying the ball behind the giant form of right tackle, Rammer Norton. Suddenly, Norton wasn't there anymore and six other guys were. He tried to shift his field. Too late. He went down hard, caught and twisted between defensive players above and below. There was a sudden wrenching, a blinding pain in the small of his back, followed by unconsciousness.

He came to as they carried him off the field. Rammer Norton was beside him, bending low. His whispered words belied the look of deep concern he wore for the others, "That'll teach ya to fuck me out of a chance at the big money!"

Thus his athletic career ended because of two compressed discs that occasionally pinched a nerve and left one or both legs numb and useless. It doomed not only a pro-football future, but likewise robbed him of his enjoyment of nearly all competitive sports. After graduation and six months of therapy, his back was pronounced healed—as long as he never wrestled or played football again. There was a brief flirtation with a job as an investigator for International Credit Corporation, then the army:

The PSA 727 was nearing LA International. His thoughts had wound their way back to the present and his doubtful future. Yes, his career was at an end. So was the war. And there was nothing to look forward to. He sat back, stifling an involuntary outcry at the pain caused by the sudden movement. As he rode down through the clouds, toward the waiting City of Angels, Mark Hardin did not realize that his war was just beginning....

1

ASHES TO ASHES

Dawn was still a half-hour away. Darkness filled the lower reaches of a small side canyon in the Topanga Canyon area of Los Angeles County. A ground-level chill hugged the chaparral, despite the fact it was July, one of the hotter months of the year. The moon had long ago set and the brighter stars had orbited away to the west, making the darkness at the bottom of the arroyo nearly total. If it hadn't been for the fantastic light-gathering properties of the Williams wide-field 4X scope, the man lying in the brush would not have been able to distinguish his target.

Mark Hardin—six-feet-two inches of lean length, one-hundred-eighty pounds of tightly controlled explosive force—lay just over the inside slope, looking down at the man and car parked in the center of a fire lane that had been cut through the courtesy of the California

Division of Forestry. He eased his aching body without moving the compact Ruger .44 Magnum carbine to which the scope was attached. Despite three weeks of concentrated effort, he was still stiff and sore. Resettled now, he checked the scope. Everything remained as before. Mark grunted his satisfaction.

As he continued to observe, Mark's mind wandered back over the days and weeks. Strange images floated through his conscious mind—images of a misty, indistinct father and mother he had never really known. There was a vision of a girl, Donna Morgan, laughing, her bright hair a swirl around her shoulders, her eyes sparkling as she ran to his arms. Other scenes crowded his mind: hoods and whispered conversations and heroin, cars roaring through the night, dueling side by side on a midnight strip of highway up by Big Bear Lake. There was the final scene of screeching tires, twisting, swirling space, bone-smashing contact, fire and death. Donna Morgan's death. He could see her again, her mangled body in a mangled car, halfway down the steep side of a barren slope of a California mountain.

There was nothing strange about what he was doing, Mark reflected. He'd done it a hundred times before in Vietnam. Penetrate the enemy's position, determine his plan of action and then strike swiftly, taking out as many key men as possible and turning well-laid plans for victory into bloody defeat. But this was July 1973, in Los Angeles County, California, U.S.A. That other war, what had been his war, was eight thousand miles and many months away. The cease-fire was nearly seven-months old, the prisoners returned and the MIAs accounted for. Final, lasting, peace Agreements were being signed even now. Yet Mark Hardin had come home, battered and broken in body and spirit, only to find this new, far more sinister enemy. As he snuggled the Ruger carbine to his cheek and shoulder, he realized he was as fully committed to this bizarre war as he had been to that distant, futile struggle. Mark jerked his attention back to the present as the man below stirred restlessly and lit a cigarette.

Boredom and a faint uneasiness, was getting to the man leaning against the sleek front fender of the bright red Ferrari GT. He felt creepy in the large, empty space. The predawn quiet of this uninhabited gully, the spicy rich aroma of dew-moistened vegetation, and the distant call of a mockingbird were all wasted on city-born-and-bred Charlie "The Horse" Cavallera. Originally from the Lower East Side in overcrowded Manhattan, Charlie The Horse had not ventured outside the teeming sprawl of greater Los Angeles in the twenty years he had been here. Trees and grass and open air, all that shit, were for farmers. Charlie was truly at home only when his feet were firmly planted on concrete.

Charlie "The Horse" Cavallera was Mafia through and through. He had come up in one of the "First Families" of New York, then moved to the coast and opened a small book that grew over the years to a position of trust and power, second only to his patron, Don Pietro Scarelli. Until just three months ago, Charlie "The Horse" had been in charge of all the Family bookie operations from Ventura County south to the Mexican border. It was a position he had fought for, and one that brought with it much respect; he was a Capo de tutti Regime, which brought as much respect as that befitting and expected for Don Pietro himself.

It was because of the respect that even he must render to his Don, that he found himself in this godforsaken place. Bitterly, he lit another Marlboro. Three months ago, Don Pietro had called him to the mansion in Beverly Hills and informed him of a new operation that was opening up. A sure thing, involving only wholesaling, it was just too good to pass up. For a long time, Don Pietro had kept himself and all his underlings clear of the drug market. With Mexico so close at hand, the drug freaks could supply themselves with little effort and they made the profit-to-risk ratio unattractive. Now, it was different. Things had changed.

The leonine features of the old Mafia Don were alive with greed as he described the operation to Charlie Cavallera. "A sure thing, goomba, so easy. All we do is receive the goods, cut it and wholesale it to the contacts who will be coming in from all over the country. Predigioso, paisan, like magic! No need to set up our own pushers, contacts, no competition in the market." The old man sighed deeply. "Millions we stand to make. All we invest is a few hundred Gs, and we make ten, fifteen times that on each load. And no sweat from the bulls, Carlo. The grease is in all the way to the top. Even the Feds can't get a. handle on this operation. Immunity, my boy," he whispered cryptically. "Im-mu-nit-ty."

Okay, so it was a good shot, a sweet operation that would net more millions into the numbered Swiss accounts that belonged to the sleek, nattily dressed old man who bossed a major portion of Southern California from his secret throne of power. Then came the joker in the deck. "And, there's no one else I can trust to handle this thing, Carlo. You must, I insist. You must handle the operation. Just you, Carlo mio. You still have a handle on that construction company? Good. It's time the boys out there on our payroll started returning something for their dough. Set it up…And you run it."

After three months in the operation, Charlie The Horse wasn't so sure he appreciated Don Pietro's "favor." After all, drugs just weren't his thing. Now, the ponies he understood—a needle here, a pill there; use. a little muscle on the jocks from time to time to keep them in line. Simple. Run a clean, profitable book, lay off the big favorites, grease the right fuzz and everything comes out right. But this was something else, the screwiest setup he had ever heard of.

Most of all, as so-called head of the operation, he disliked what he was doing right now, acting as nothing more than an errand boy. He picked up the stuff, took it to a tame chemist at Valley College in San Fernando—who cut it and repackaged it—then he took it to the drop, where the messengers from back East came in one by one to leave thick stacks of bills and take away the powdered happiness. Just an errand boy, he even took the stacks of money to Don Pietro—albeit for four percent of the action.

And he didn't like the Chinaman. That was the screwiest thing about the whole screwy operation. Every time Charlie The Horse made a pickup in the presence of the Chinaman, his skin crawled. Never a word: not a hello, good-bye or kiss my ass. There was something un-American about the Chinaman...no, not un-American, maybe non-American. Yeah, that was better.

Charlie Cavallera shivered in the predawn cold and lit another cigarette. His thoughts turned to the rumor that the local fuzz, or perhaps the Feds—regardless of what Don Pietro had assured him—had penetrated his operation. "So what if they had?" he snorted aloud. His boys had taken care of that problem three weeks before. That nosy punk and the broad. Over the edge of-the canyon and down the side. No one had survived, according to the report. Chalk up another one for the hazardous back road to Big Bear. No fuzz action since and everyone riding the aerie for word of a nosy newcomer. Simple as that. Charlie The Horse was smugly proud of the fact that nobody, but nobody, could penetrate an operation he was in charge of...and live.

On the hillside, Mark Hardin used the glow of Charlie's cigarette to make minute final adjustments on his weapon. His thoughts turned again to Donna Morgan, and grief quickly fanned to smoldering anger, growing hotter and threatening to burst into flame. He nursed it, drawing sustenance from it, gaining the strength to wait, wait for the right moment.

Just when dawn sent pale light onto the higher hills,

making an imperceptible—but adequate—change in the illumination of the scene below, the thrumming throb of a helicopter drew Mark Hardin's attention to the air above the opposite slope.

Locustlike, skittering sideways through the dawn-lit air, a small chopper came into view. Pink rays of sunrise refracted off the Plexiglas bubble, making it impossible for Mark to determine the number of occupants.

This was an unexpected development. Mark was not deterred. Light had not yet penetrated his initial point and, dressed in dark clothing, his olive skin further darkened by burnt cork, he was just another of many dark clumps of greasewood and sage.

The chopper hovered over the fold in the earth for several seconds, while Charlie The Horse rushed to the driver's side of his Ferrari and blinked his lights in the prearranged signal. Then it slid downward, sideways, to land softly in a huge billow of Southern California caliche dust. The rotating wings wound down to a stop as the dust dissipated. Charlie withdrew a large attaché case from the back seat of his car and rested it on the long hood of his car.

From the chopper emerged a short, stocky figure. He crossed quickly to where Charlie waited for him. It was the Chinaman. Mutual dislike was evident on both faces, as the Chinaman inspected the contents of the attaché case. He nodded curt approval of the stacks of crisp bills. Arrogant bastard, Charlie thought, he didn't even bother to count it. Without a word, the Chinaman turned his back on Charlie and returned to the chopper.

Behind his back, Charlie thrust a single stiff finger in the air in a gesture of contempt.

Through the wide field of his Williams 4X scope, Mark Hardin had also observed the contents of the attaché case—neat stacks of one-hundred-dollar bills, tightly bound in brown-paper bank collars. His eyes widened in surprise. This was a bigger deal than he had anticipated; a grin of satisfaction spread, over his face. He eased his position, to allow the big .44 Mag to swing where he wanted it to point. Not moving the alignment of his sight, Mark tracked Charlie as he closed the attaché case and moved away from his car toward the chopper. Things couldn't be better for Mark.

They met halfway, the Chinaman seemed unperturbed by the Mafioso's open hostility. He was carrying ten kilos of pure heroin. He put it down and reached for the attaché case.

Gently, ever so gently, Mark took up the last of the slack in the smoothly honed trigger. The big gun roared and bucked, but Charlie The Horse Cavallera did not hear it. The speeding, 248-grain, soft-tipped bullet easily beat the sound to the target. It took Charlie just slightly left of and three millimeters above his right eye. Crashing impact threw him away like a rag doll, taking with it most of the back of his skull. He didn't even live long enough to reflect on the startling fact that a penetrator had indeed reached the very top of his operation.

Mark swung slightly to his right, tracking until he centered on the Chinese, who had remained frozen for a fatal split second at the edge of the wide-field scope.

Mark stitched him with two shots, the first was a bull's-eye through the breastbone, the second sizzled through his gut to remove a large portion of spine.

Quickly, Mark shifted his weapon again, this time to the chopper, which was trying to gain the air. His fourth shot splintered the bubble canopy, barely missing the pilot, but lending urgency to his efforts. The fragile bird lifted. Mark wasted only two more shots, both hits, but not fatal. The six-shot box magazine on the specially altered Ruger was empty, and he used his dwindling time to get a close-up of the serial numbers of the chopper for future reference.

He was fifty-one seconds into the hit.

As the chopper gained altitude to make its escape over the ridge, Mark carefully policed his area, picking up his brass and removing every trace of his presence. Then, as the whirlybird sped out of sight to safety, he broke cover and headed down hill, taking time to wipe out his footprints. He moved as if he had all the time in the world. The men in the gully were in no hurry.

Mark allowed himself a tight grin of triumph and a deep, satisfying breath. He had a flash of regret that he had decided to stop smoking when he began the demanding regimen of his current training program.

His lips were still white-rimmed with anger, and his words seemed more spat at the corpses at his feet than spoken. "That's two for Donna. Ninety-eight to go."

He moved away from the sprawled bodies, making several trips to and from the sleek Ferrari, mixing his own footprints with the others to add to the confusion that would come later, when this was reported. On his last trip, he paused to check the dead Chinese. His search revealed just what he had expected; there was not a single piece of identification in any of the pockets of the dead man's clothes, nor were there labels or laundry marks. He completed his final trip to the Ferrari, bringing along the attaché case. He had decided beforehand to leave the heroin behind as a little teaser for the police. A puzzler that should spur them to action. Mark Hardin set the case of money carefully on the floor behind the driver's seat, and followed it with his "old reliable" .44 Magnum. He got into the car and hit the ignition.

A low, deep-throated, rumbling filled the silent morning air as the Ferrari responded, each of its eight cylinders gulping gas from the carburetor. Then Mark set the hand brake and climbed out. He removed his black-and-brown splotched dark green jump suit, revealing a clean, if wrinkled, pair of avocado-green walking shorts, white-and-green knit shirt, and matching green socks and deck shoes. From a zipper pocket of the coverall-type working suit, he got a small vial of cleanser and a wad of tissues. Working quickly, he rubbed the blacking from his face and hands. Then he dropped the cleaning gear into the car and ran comb like fingers through his modishly cut black hair. He looked at himself in the sideview mirror and was satisfied with his ablutions.

Mark cut the wheels of the big machine, tooling it in a tight arc and heading down the fire lane toward a dirt road that would eventually take him to a hard-surfaced state highway. CBS Studio Ranch, where Matt Dillon felled the bad guys with a six-gun full of blanks on the Gunsmoke set lay on the other side of several ridges. Behind him, Mark left a scene of violence where the bullets were real and the blood didn't come in a bottle from Bud Westmore. Full light was just breaking, harsh and bright against the tinder-dry brush hills.

As he drove with an increasing skill, learning the quirks of the sweet foreign job, Mark's head was filled with questions regarding the new and unexplained facts he had acquired in the blitzing few minutes of his hit on Charlie The Horse.

First, there was the very large amount of money, now happily in his possession, that was to be exchanged for a shipment of heroin larger and—from his brief, inexpert examination—more pure than anything he had ever imagined. Who had the dough to lay that much out twice a month and keep his other operations running? And there had never been a whisper of a new source, bigger scores on the streets or anything to indicate that Charlie Cavallera was entering the retail market with so much pure dream dust.

Then there was the unexpected purity of the heroin. No known source was presently providing wholesalers with anything nearly as pure as this ten-kilo load. No wonder the big payoff. At street prices, that dream dust would have been worth three or four times any other supply.

And the sterile Chinaman—no identifying labels or

papers, armed with a 9mm Luger pistol, dressed in clothing of several different nations' manufacture—all of it suggested a connection to someone's espionage apparel, but whose? And why dealing in dope?

Not to forget the chopper—everything that flew had to file a flight plan. What was the cover that allowed this detour to deliver the Chinaman and his "H"?

The questions came thick and fast. He relegated them to the back of his mind, storing them away for consideration when he reached his destination, far to the east in the Calico Mountains.

Mark made one stop before hitting the freeway to Barstow. From the outskirts of Chatsworth, near Hopeville, he called the sheriff's substation nearest Topanga Canyon, to report the shooting.

"A whole lot of shooting, officer. Sounded like a regular war. Oh, my yes, up there in Topanga Canyon." He used his Mr. Peepers voice, which was how the desk sergeant later described it. Mark hung up quickly before more questions were asked.

Back in the late Charlie Cavallera's Ferrari, Mark made a mental apology to the shade of the late Wally Cox for the voice disguise.

Bumping and grinding slowly over the rutted road to The Stronghold—Professor Haskins' home, deep in the Calico Mountains—Mark began to lament his means of escape. The low-slung Ferrari had no business being here in the arid, rocky region of California's desert mountain range. Each bump and jolt of the old track—

cut nearly a hundred years before by the wide-tired, heavy borax wagons and their twenty-mule teams—sent hot spears of pain through his tired body. Always slim, there was little save hard muscle and sinew to pad the bones of Mark's long, spare frame. Half a night without sleep and the rapid fire morning of killing had sapped what little strength Mark had to spare, and now his vision swam before him; rock and cacti, sky and mountain whirled around and icy sweat oozed from every pore. Through it all, Mark's dogged will dragged him along.

At last Mark Hardin reached the macadam drive that lead to the cool garage at its end. The car leaped forward to be quickly engulfed by the interior of the underground hillside garage. He gave a final touch to the accelerator and cut off the roar in midblast. Cranking down his window, he let the dry coolness of the garage replace the dank, parlor car artificiality of automobile air conditioning.

Safe at least, Mark let the fatigue sweep over him for a few moments. He closed his eyes and slumped forward, until his forehead touched the cool leather of the steering wheel. The effect of fatigue on his still unhealed body played merry hell with his system, lulling him toward much-needed sleep. Each twinge reminded him of the self-induced torture of forcing his overtaxed body to the adrenaline-charged activity of a split-second hit. Well, he'd done it again and again in 'Nam, for a lot less noble cause, why not here? The enemy might be different, but they were just as slimy.

The stakes were the same. It felt so good to rest to let the tension, pain and gut-wrenching fear seep out of his body....

Swiftly and silently, the old man with the knife was nearly upon Mark before he could react.

2

AFTER ACTION REPORT

David Red Eagle's moccasins made no sound as he moved to the glittering machine that Mark had acquired in the course of his grim duty. Yet, as he closed the last few steps, he found himself looking down the deadly muzzle of Mark's .45 Colt Commander. The click of the safety was the loudest sound in the world. The sho-tu-ca medicine, which Mark was still learning, never let him completely relax.

Not a hair turned, no twitch of muscle or blink of obsidian, button eyes betrayed whatever emotions brewed within the old Indian's head. "He, he, ha! Hokka he, ha!" he grunted softly in Cheyenne. "Look, look. It is a good day to die! You are back, little brother? Wah zazhe ith ca ha."

"He, ha. Ith ca ha! And the Great Spirit be with you too, grandfather." Even as he spoke, Mark wondered at the highly civilized politeness that was inherent in the language of his forebears—a language, he was now learning for the first time. This old man, David Red Eagle, was in no way related to him, but custom and courtesy required the reverential address of grandfather.

A smile creased the wrinkled old face, "You learn quickly and well, my son. But," he continued in Cheyenne, "your face shows signs of great weariness. Come, quickly, we will give you life."

From the outside, no one would ever have guessed a house existed in this rugged country. True, there was the strip of macadam—beginning abruptly and ending nowhere—but the desert behind the San Bernardino Mountains was filled with similar strips from land development schemes that had never gotten off the ground. Subdivision stakes, followed by a short strip of paving and an office in a trailer, some flapping colored plastic flags and there it was: Instant Land Promotion, California-style. Some had made it big, others had not. No, no one familiar with the ups and downs of California land promotions would find the mile-and-a-quarter macadam strip cause for curiosity. Professor Haskins had the ideal hideaway.

The crusty old professor of geology and minerals, now retired from the faculty of the University of Southern California, had built wisely and well, making sure of his privacy—from a world he deemed gone mad —by locating in one of the many abandoned borax mines that dotted the Calico Mountains. Using native stone and adobe mud, the above ground portions of the house blended perfectly into the surrounding terrain, so much so that one could nearly fall through a recessed picture window before realizing it was there.

The remainder of his house: a small lab, kitchen, theater, art gallery, library and bedrooms—ten of them; for although the professor thought the world insane, he had many friends who came for lengthy visits—was built into the shafts, stopes and tunnels of the old mine.

It was into one of these that David Red Eagle led the exhausted Mark Hardin. This was a special place, built by the old Indian to heal him from the effects of the Mafia-induced auto accident that had claimed the life of Donna Morgan, Professor Haskins' niece, and left Mark for a dead man on a mountainside far from The Stronghold. Well down the tunnel, near its junction with a deep, flooded shaft, was built a sweat lodge—exact in every detail to those used a century before by Mark's ancestors for puberty rites and purification rituals. Mark could see from the small wisp of smoke as it was drawn rapidly off and up an adjacent shaft by a strong draft, that Red Eagle had been preparing for him.

He shucked off his clothes and stood naked before the entrance. The old man mumbled ritual words that were only half heard, and less understood; by Mark. Raising his arms, he invoked the aid of the Great Spirit. Then he signaled that Mark should enter.

The inside was illuminated by a ruddy glow, emanating from a deep, round bed of glowing coals in the center of the skin-and-cedar lodge. Over the top of the coals was a lattice-work basket of iron strips; holding a number of small round stones. Mark sat Indian style, cross-legged, as close to the fire as he could. Then David Red Eagle threw water onto the stones, scooped from a hide bucket with a gourd ladle. Steam rose, filling the close air of the skin tent with moist warmth. It was better than a sauna or Turkish bath, scented by wood smoke and the sweet medicine herbs that Red Eagle now sprinkled over the rocks and fire below.

Mark breathed deeply, filling his lungs with the hot, moist air and pungent odor of the herbs. Fully believing in the healing properties of the herbal vapors he was inhaling, his mind-began to relax his body. More small sticks were added to the fire, followed by more water, steam, and another round of herbs. Mark's breathing slowed, became deep and rhythmic. His eyes looked far beyond the moment; beyond the fire; beyond the old man who crouched on the other side of it, mumbling and sprinkling dried leaves and grasses on the hot stones; beyond even the skin walls of the lodge. He was seeking, as he had been taught, communion with the Great Spirit, creator of all things in this universe. Maker of the buffalo and the horse and of the Red Man. Yes, even creator of the white ones, from whose bloodlines Mark likewise had sprung.

An hour sped by, leaving Mark relaxed in body but still seething in spirit. His thoughts went back to the time he had first come here, a bruised and battered hulk. After his discharge from Letterman General. Hospital and from the army, Mark had drifted aimlessly through Southern California, to the only home he knew, the teeming basin of Greater Los Angeles, with its seven million buck-hustling, smog-breathing souls. Even that wasn't a real home. Mark thought wryly of the foster "homes" of his youth; people attracted by the seventy-five dollars per-kid, per-month extra to booze it up with. The money was offered by the county to take care of the homeless waifs that filled the county orphanage and the juvenile detention hall. Hustled from the aloof and forbidding to the licentious and permissive, so to speak, Mark Hardin had never known a home until the middle years of his adolescence, so it was not a homing instinct that drew him south from San Francisco, rather it was the listless wandering of the wounded. Soul-sick and weary, he had come at last to Los Angeles and from there to the home of his former football coach at UCLA.

It had been Ted Stoner, that same coach, who had first suggested Mark get off the booze and brawling routine and get himself put back together out in the desert at the home of an old and dear friend, Professor Willard Haskins. The old teacher, too renowned in his field of geology and too rich to be called eccentric, lived alone—Stoner informed Mark—out in the Calico Mountains. He had a dream house he called The Stronghold, built into a hillside. It was always open to company, especially of the broken wing variety.

Mark fought the idea at first, but Stoner insisted

and one day he drove Mark out there himself. Stoner had obviously discussed Mark's problem with the old professor in advance, for the old man took over at once. He issued orders and instructions as if he were commanding a division in the field. He would hear not a word of protest from Mark. It was settled, simple as that. Mark would move into one of the many bedrooms in his underground stronghold.

After only a week of lying outside, exposing his body to the burning rays of the desert sun, alternating with soaking sessions in an icy underground pool, Mark was up and around without the constant twinges of pain that had sapped his mental powers and efforts at recuperation. He was even able to smile and enjoy the rare steaks prepared by his host, and served with salads, as well as frothy glasses, of Carlsberg Elephant Stout, and king-size Irish whiskey. Life, he decided, could be sweet—at least for a while.

Yet one problem remained unresolved. He was no longer able to do the bending twisting, stooping activities he was so long accustomed to doing with his hard, well-tuned athlete's body. This more than anything else, served to keep his spirits low and his regeneration from completion. It took the arrival of David Red Eagle to alter this downward course.

He came, seemingly, out of nowhere. A gnarled and grizzled old Indian, tramping the desert to all points of the compass. His leathery, wrinkled Indian face gave no clue to his age, but he had been born in California some time after his family was relocated there from the upper reservation following the Wounded Knee Massacre. He was Cheyenne, he maintained proudly, and gifted with all the medicine secrets of his beautiful people. From almost the first moment he had laid eyes on Mark, his high cheekbones, dark hair and shoe-button eyes, set in a wide face of strong, features and prominent hawk nose, the old man refused to address him in anything but the Cheyenne language. "He is one of the Beautiful People," he said in singular explanation to Willard Haskins.

So strong was his insistence that Mark Hardin was Cheyenne that he drew out of the younger man as much as Mark knew of his own past. Never satisfied with Mark's autobiography, the old Indian grunted to himself and set off on his plan. First, he took over the treatment of Mark's physical ills. He hunted for deer in the distant San Bernardino Mountains, and the Fish and Game Department be damned about seasons, bringing back in his battered old pickup truck the meat and hides. He fed the liver, tongue and choicest steaks to Mark Hardin, using the brains to cure the hides, from which he built the sweat lodge. He even began to teach Mark the Cheyenne language.

All of this made a pleasant, belly-filling diversion, so Mark went along, amused at first, then taking it more and more seriously as his physical aches began to leave him through the ministrations of the old man. David Red Eagle merely grunted in guttural Cheyenne and continued to work on his living clay, sculpting from it what he saw there.

It took a different medicine than that mumbled and dispensed by David Red Eagle to bring about the final revitalization of Mark Hardin. About two and a half months after Mark first came to The Stronghold, Professor Willard Haskins received a visit from his niece, Miss Donna Morgan. In addition to overwhelming good looks, coupled with a pixie-like sense of humor and an alarming capacity for her uncle's Irish whiskey, Donna Morgan was also a research anthropologist, working on the American Indian cultures at the USC Department of Anthropology.

She studied Mark closely in daylight and at night. Then, after long, lip pursing and head shaking contemplation—a shaking that swirled her hair in an enchanting and seductive manner never before seen, but greatly enjoyed by Mark—she pronounced Red Eagle to be one-hundred-percent accurate in his evaluation.

"Face it, mister," she told Mark, as she brought him a refill of his Danish stout. "Somewhere in your family's past there was an aborigine in the fuel supply. In breech clout, braids and feathers, you'd be a dead ringer for Crazy Horse."

Mark was stunned, not so much by this pronouncement, as by the presence of the petite, perky Donna Morgan. He agreed to accompany her back to the city for a search of his background to learn what they could. They found that Mark had been orphaned at four years of age in a head-on collision that had claimed the lives of his parents, two older brothers, and a sister two years younger. Funny, he had always thought of himself as just an orphan. His mother was of German and Cheyenne ancestry, his father a Welshman. They began to look into other things: the present whereabouts of Rammer Norton, who had been responsible for Mark's first back injury, which led them to Charlie The Horse. Then one thing led to another until that night when....

"Out!" commanded David Red Eagle.

Mark sprang lightly to his feet and ran from the lodge to dive deeply into the oily black waters of the underground spring that filled the shaft.

His head broke the surface and, with quick, silent strokes, he swam twenty-five lengths. Short though they were, the contrast to the lethargic heat exhilarated him. Then, springing from the icy water, Mark ran out the mouth of the tunnel into the hot, dry air of late afternoon on the desert. His skin dried quickly as he ran six laps of the macadam drive: a total of seven-and-a-half miles. The tough, callused soles of his feet registered little of the egg-frying heat of the softened blacktop and, at the end of his run, his body was coated with a light, healthy sheen of moisture. His breathing was deep and heavy, yet even, despite the hour of exertion.

Back inside the tunnel, he rubbed down with bunches of sweetgrass, brought down from the high mountain valleys. Then he dressed in moccasins, calf-length leather trousers of soft doeskin and a beaded, open vest—Red Eagle's idea of proper leisure clothes.

Mark and the old Indian climbed the spiral stairs to the ground-level portion of Professor Haskins' stronghold.

"Ah, there you are, my boy!" Professor Haskins stood in darkness, silhouetted against the brightness let in by the large, recessed, picture window of nonreflecting glass. A fringe of white hair stood out, halo like, from his head. He crossed the intervening, space with short, silent steps, extending in one hand a huge glass, tinkling with ice and filled with a pale amber fluid. "Here's what you need...Fix you up in no time."

"One. Remember, only one," Red Eagle admonished, before leaving to attend to dinner.

Mark examined the Texas shot glass and then the man who had become host, mentor and coconspirator. He raised the glass. "L'chaim!" he toasted and downed a respectable quantity of chilled Irish whiskey.

"To life and health," mused the older man.

"A teammate of mine at UCLA, Bernie Schwartz, used it all the time. The VC ambushed a patrol he was leading in 'Nam. Cut him down like a weed." He drank again. The mellow liquor rushed to his head, its effect magnified by the strenuous exercise and a day without food.

For the better part of an hour, Mark and Willard Haskins discussed his condition, state of training, and everything but what happened earlier that day. There was a quiet quality of anticipation in the manner of the older man, yet he did not make an effort to broach the subject. All in due time, he knew.

They went outdoors for dinner, to a shaded area that

overlooked the wide expanse of desert. Red Eagle brought his own plate and joined them. Mark fell to his food with a will: steaks—thick slabs of meat cooked blood-rare over an open fire of manzanita and white oak, half a head of lettuce for Mark, and boiled yucca shoots for everyone.

"...so, everything except that chopper getting away, went according to plan. If we had known about it earlier, I could have taken it out too." Mark was winding up his narration of the day's events.

"And the money?" inquired the Professor.

Mark opened the attach case, placing it on the low table that sat before the wide expanse of glass where the nightly drama of change was being played out, the red and purple hues of a desert sunset giving away to the splendor of stars. With widening eyes, the three men counted their day's take. Two hundred thousand dollars! It was a figure beyond belief. Combined with the war chest donated by his two patrons, it placed Mark in a position to wreak havoc on any aspect of the crime scene he chose.

"About that chopper, Professor," Mark interrupted their contemplations. "You should be able to check out the registration more easily than anyone else. Would you go into town tomorrow and look it up?"

"Of course, of course. Two hundred thousand. It's time to think in bigger terms than revenge, my boy. It's time to..." Willard Haskins' voice faded off into his dreams of victory over organized crime and corruption.

"Before too much time gets by, I want to change the

color of that Ferrari and get safe license plates, but that can-wait. I still have the RX-3," Mark thought aloud.

"Next," Professor Haskins asked at last, returning to the immediate situation. "Where do you hit them next?

"I'll let them tell me that," came Mark's sardonic reply.

3

DAMAGE REPORT

LIGHTS BLAZED IN THE PALATIAL MANSION occupied by Peter Scarelli—born Pietro Scarelli, in Trenton, New Jersey, sixty-five years before—far up on Westwood Drive in Beverly Hills. Cars had been arriving all evening and any nosy neighbors—there weren't any among the economic level represented by this prestigious neighborhood—would have merely concluded that another of Pete's parties was under way, with its bevy of starlets, press representatives and financial wheels. This particular gathering, however, was for a far more sinister purpose than outward appearance would have led one to believe.

"The goddamned cops got the shipment, the goddamned contact gets blown in the weeds and now you tell me something that maybe I don't already know? That these hotshot hit boys have the goddamned money, the car and Charlie Cavallera dead! Like my own son, he was, and they snuff him like that," Don

Pietro Scarelli shouted, slamming his hand on the desk with a sharp report to emphasize his words. His vigorous activity, high color and blazing eyes belied his sixty-five years. His gray hair was the only mark of his age, and that was well-groomed and glowing with healthy life. He turned his wrath on the men before him once again. "Buncha fuckin' wise guys I have working for me. Santa Maria, stupido..." he launched into a tirade of fluid Sicilian profanity, calling on the saints to witness the incompetence of his underlings. When it wore itself out, he took a long pull from a glass of ice water and collected his thoughts.

"Stan," he said to Stan "The Man" Ollivetti, a thick, stocky man of some forty years, whose expensive suit set off his darkly handsome features.

"You take a crew, get over to Charlie's place and take over for the time being. Get out the cars and let's run this bunch to ground. Nobody who's in the know will believe that crap on the tube about a rival gang. We know better. So, we gotta find these cute amateurs and chill them fast. Make an object lesson of 'em that nobody, but nobody will ever forget."

"Sure it ain't just some grabby cop got the dough?" Stan The Man asked his superior.

"And that flashy red bomb The Horse drove, too? Hell no, use your brain if you got one. Only an amateur or a real dumb pro would boost a set of wheels like that. You find them! No excuses, just by God find them!"

The discreet ting-ting of a bell-chime interrupted a further tirade from the Mafia Don? His hand grabbed a yellow telephone on his desk. As he lifted it to his ear, his features changed, softened and his tone of voice was respectful. "Yes, sir."

From the other end, came the muted tones of an upper-class English accent—so polished as to seem like an accomplished actor doing Lord Dunhill. "Yes, sir. We're on it right now...Yes, sir, I can understand why you are most upset. What about me? I lost my number-two man, a boy as dear to me as a son...No, sir. I am not allowing emotion to determine the next move...I have a very competent associate taking charge in the field...Yes, sir. I'm sorry, sir. We...we were wondering...ah, now that the liaison man has been...Oh, you are, sir! Yes, sir, that is good news, very good news, sir. Thank you, sir. I assure you my men are on it and will have results within forty-eight hours ...." They goddamned better, he thought. "Thank you, sir. Good night."

Don Pietro Scarelli replaced the receiver in its cradle and sat down, reaching for his ice water again.

"That," he said without necessity, "was His Lordship."

"And?" asked Stan "The Man" and several others in one voice.

"He's setting up a new contact. One Week and business as usual. But," he turned his attention to Olivetti, "he expects to see results from us and soon. You get out there and get on it, Stan."

The top capo left to Don Pietro's empire turned to leave as the yellow phone rang again. Don Pietro signaled him to wait.

"Hope I didn't interrupt anything important, old boy," came the voice over the wire. "Just received a reliable piece of information from the local constabulary out there. Seems they had reports of a red Ferrari on the road as far as the edge of your bleeding desert. Nothing else. Do hope it helps. Also, your contact will be set as I mentioned, six nights from now…and tell the lads good hunting. Ta-ta."

Don Pietro was impressed. Even his own inside men had not reported anything this pertinent. Whoever "His Lordship," as their unknown contact had been dubbed by Charlie The Horse knew in official circles, he had a lot more pull than the aging Don. "That was His Lordship again. Says the delivery will be on six days from now. Also said that whoever pulled the hit drove Charlie's car out into the desert and disappeared. That's a job for von Richtohfen and his windmill. Send some of their boys out to the construction site and get him off early tomorrow." After all the underlings had departed, save his personal bodyguard and members of the household staff, Don Pietro changed from ice water to bourbon, pouring a healthy slug. He downed half of it in a gulp, raised his glass in a silent tribute to the late Charlie Cavallera. The yellow phone rang a third time. Don Pietro was accustomed to dealing with His Lordship in such a manner; several brief phone conversations he bet they each came from a different phone—over a period of an evening or midday to complete a single piece of business. Sighing, he reached for the instrument.

"By the way," came the same cultured tones, "our associates in this venture insisted that you make good on the loss of the merchandise."

"What!" The idea of Don Pietro having to pay for the drugs he had not received, not once but twice, drove all deference from his voice. "Whaddahell you talking? I make up for the lost money? Hell, I lost the money, the shipment and my very best man in that deal and this supplier, a mere shipper of goods wants me to pay for it? No! Not only no, but hell no!"

"I'm afraid it's a bit more complicated than that, old boy," came the soft voice. "I'm sorry to say, the price of continued operations is just precisely that...No argument, no negotiations. Pay for the loss incurred by the shipper or no more business. In fact, old boy, he insisted on payment first, whether or not business continued."

Don Pietro was furious. "Why, the crooked bastard! Just who in hell is this smart-ass who thinks he can boss around the head of a Family like this?"

"Now, now," placated the disembodied voice.

"Remember the agreement. No names, no identifications at any time."

"Fuck the agreement! I won't pay. No! No way will I pay!"

"Then I am afraid you are out of the wholesale business."

Those icy words, delivered without emotion, stopped the fiery old Don. He thought a long while into the silent phone,

"I say, are you there?" came a query from the other end.

"Hell yes, I'm here. Gimme a second to think, okay?" His mind raced, weighing the factors. Charlie had always insisted on a change in procedure. He wanted a couple of button men along. Maybe, just maybe. "Ah, Your Lordship, ah...you know, I think this is a pretty good reason for bringing up what my man said before, you know, about a security arrangement. Well, ah, I'm willing to meet this supplier halfway. Remember, he's the one who insisted none of my boys go along. Well, they didn't and-we lost a shipment. So, what about this? If we can have more than one guy, not an army understand, but two or three along for protection of the shipment, then I can see payin' maybe...half...of the loss. After all, if we had had some boys there, this wouldn't have happened. As matter stand, we both lost on this thing, right? So what's he got to lose this way?"

There was an equally long pause on the other end. "I think I can speak for our other associate to this extent. He will approve of the half payment. I'll have to consult him and notify you about the other. Sleep well, old boy." And he was gone, just like that.

That night, Don Pietro Scarelli didn't sleep well at all.

4

DUST TO DUST

FOR WHAT SEEMED THE THOUSANDTH TIME THAT morning, the telephone jangled again. "Sheriff's substation, Sergeant Patterson," answered the man behind the desk. There was a static-like squawking from the other end. "Hell yes, I know we're up to our necks in a murder. And I know we've been sitting on it for more than twenty-four hours. I just got the autopsy reports." More squawking. "Sure, you have a deadline to meet, Shaun, but right now all I can say is that we found two guys shot full of very big holes. Give me an hour and we'll have a press release. Bye." The stocky redhead replaced the phone in its cradle and turned his attention to the reports lying on his desk. He pulled a cigarette from the pocket of his lime-green, broad-collar dress shirt and lit it absently.

As his eyes flicked over the first report, he smiled to himself to see his own theory was being vindicated. This hit was done by a single guy. Up above the scene somewhere. The hell with what the others thought. He hadn't left a trace, sure, but he was up there all right. He'd used a .44—a big gun under any circumstances—and odds on that it was a Magnum. No doubt a Ruger .44 carbine.

Fingerprints had identified the dead Caucasian as Charles Rudolfo Cavallera, aka "Charlie The Horse." That cleared up a few things in the lab report. Whoever it was that had hit these two, he'd left the scene in Charlie's big red Ferrari GT. So much for the Michelin Radials identified from moulage casts. But why leave the heroin? The lab had said it was the most pure "H" ever taken from any source. Most street stuff was cut to less than fifteen percent pure heroin and wholesalers were finding their suppliers bringing in stuff cut as much as sixty percent with sugar. A new source? If one was to believe the glop out on the morning news, a rival gang or any band of independent hoods making this hit would have taken the smack. Was someone trying to tell them something? He read on. Outside of the readily observable loss of the back of Charlie The Horse's head, there was little in the report relating to the crime. Kelly Patterson shrugged and went on to the other report.

Now this one was something to get your teeth into. This Chinese was a complete mystery. Not a thing showing. No record of prints, no identification of any kind on the corpse and a lot to indicate—medically at least—that he was a foreigner. His concentration was interrupted by the sound of someone clearing his throat.

Standing in the doorway to Patterson's office were two men. The first, with a small grin of familiar acquaintance on his face, was George Hart, a Special Agent from the local office of the FBI. The second man was a stranger. They entered as Kelly looked up. "Mornin', Kelly. Interrupt anything particular?"

"Not really, George. Just a gangland killing, a mystery killer, and a million-dollar heroin find. Just a routine day. Have a seat. Who's, ah...?"

The other man interrupted, self-importance oozing from his voice. "Barry Taylor, State Department, Security Division. Is this room safe?"

Perhaps he shouldn't have done it, Kelly mused later. If things hadn't gotten off to that start, maybe it would have come out better. As it was, he exploded with laughter. When he quieted, a few seconds later, he looked around his familiar office with what he imagined was proper James Bond seriousness and replied, "Last time I checked, there wasn't a bug in the house, Taylor. 'Course that was the year Noah came over in the Ark."

It didn't get them off right at all. The man from the State Department was grim. "I hardly expected this, Sergeant." He made the title sound like a dirty thing. "This is a serious matter. I assure you my request is normal under the circumstances."

The guy takes himself much too seriously, Kelly thought, not at all chastened. "What circumstances, Mr. Taylor?"

"Your dead Chinese, Sergeant Patterson. Before I say anything more, it is my duty to advise you of the provisions of the National Security Act of 1921 and the National Security Act of 1943."

"I think I know what you mean. That's the law that says I can't be compelled to testify in a State court on any matter pertinent to a pending Federal case and the other thing about not being able to say anything about anything to anyone about what we talk about for a period of ten years, right?"

"Essentially," the man from the State Department sniffed, "in a crude way." He paused, then opened his briefcase and extracted a photograph. "Is this your unidentified Chinese?"

Kelly examined the photo. It was the one all right. He nodded in reply.

"I was afraid of that. Your Chinese is, I am sorry to say, a certain Kwang Luk Su...a diplomatic courier for the People's Republic of China, UN Mission," Barry Taylor informed Kelly. "He was not known to be anywhere near the West Coast, and was supposed to have departed the country. The entire matter has come as quite a shock to us, quite a shock. As a matter of fact, Sergeant, he was believed to be at the Chinese Embassy in Montreal, in French Canada. He wasn't supposed to be back in this country for several weeks. I think you can understand the predicament this places us in."

"I'm sorry, but I can't," Kelly told him candidly.

The man from State went on in his prissy manner. "This is a very delicate international situation. It could result in most unfortunate repercussions. Therefore," his watery gaze rested on the soft brown eyes of the young policeman across the desk from him, "it is necessary for me to inform you that we will handle the investigation from here on out. I have been authorized by the highest possible sources in the Department of State to demand all of the information so far developed on this crime and to request the cooperation of the Sheriff's Department in suppressing the identity of the Chinese, Kwang Luk Su, to avoid unfavorable interpretations by the press. We expect your department to withdraw entirely from the case and allow the proper authorities to handle it from here.

"We want whoever did this in the worst possible way," the Man from State intoned. "In fact, we will take complete charge of finding the man. You did say killer in the singular, didn't you? Indicating there was only one person involved, correct?" Shocked into unbelieving silence, Kelly could only nod dumbly in the affirmative. "We must find him then in the least possible time. This could create, an international incident of serious consequences. At all costs, we must not embarrass the government of the People's Republic."

"Protect this slopie drug peddler! Like hell!" Kelly snorted in the amazed faces of the government men, his disbelief now flashing into anger. "You seem to forget what he was doing at the time he died. He was in the act of transferring ten kilos of the purest heroin ever seized by any department in Southern California—or anywhere else for that matter—into the hands of one of the most powerful Capo regime's in Don Pietro's Family. And you want us to soft-peddle the thing so the slopies won't be embarrassed? Just whose State Department do you work for?"

"You don't like the Chinese very much, do you, Sergeant?" the Man from State replied with quiet nastiness.

"Like them! They shot me full of holes when I was just a kid Marine in Korea and in the last twenty-one years I've watched them get into the United Nations, an official visit by our President, then 'Most Favored Nation' status and now...now you come here and tell me that their feelings are more important than the fact that the powdered poison they are peddling is slowly killing our kids." Kelly's eyes glowed with anger, borne of dedication. "Get out of here," he continued. "You State Department types may want to handle this your own way, with kid gloves, pussyfooting around the real issue and trying to get vengeance for your Chink friends against the one who did it, but there's one fact you overlooked.

"The crime was committed within the jurisdiction of the Los Angeles County Sheriff's Department. If he was not officially in the country, on legitimate business, it is not automatically a Federal case. So, this department will handle its own investigation in its own way and will release to the press what we determine should be released. All you can think of is 'getting the guy' who might cause you and the Red Chinese some discomfort at the diplomatic tables. Hell, knowing who those two were and what it was they were doing, if I find the guy, I'd like to give him a medal.

"And don't figure you can intimidate me with that fucking National Security Act crap. As far as I am concerned, and the sheriff will back me up on it. We never heard of anything and we are pursuing our own investigation. Now, get out!"

Openmouthed, Barry Taylor stood up, snapping his briefcase and moving toward the door. He flashed a vicious look backward as Kelly went on.

"George, want to wait a minute and I'll give you Xerox copies of our reports, but get this striped-pants pandejo out of here."

Silence settled on them with the departure of the Man from State. Each was busy with his own thoughts about what had happened. Kelly buzzed for a clerk to come in; he sent out the reports to be copied. He lit another smoke and smiled tentatively at the FBI man.

"Well, George, I made a hell of a mess of that. Sorry, but every time I get a case involving drugs, I sort of go out of my mind. You ever seen a ten-year-old addict?" he asked absently. "A scrawny, haunted kid who would sell his sister's body—or his own—for money to buy a fix? Goddamn it! No cover-up this time. No fine senator or governor's, kid kicking up his heels. A Red Chinese diplomat dealing heroin to the Mafia and I'm on the case." He changed, abruptly. "George, you'll see it in my reports, but did you stop to think? Why did whoever pulled this job leave that "H" behind? The most pure smack ever and he leaves it. I was thinking; when you two came in, maybe the guy left it for us...shake us up a little, you know. Make us think?"

George Hart studied his fingernails a few moments. "Look into it, Kelly. Give the whole thing hell." His smile held no humor, only a distant sadness. "I was at Inchon, with the Navy, helping take you poor bastards off after the fiasco at the reservoir. Screw the State Department. Find out about the heroin and we'll find out about the slaughter out there yesterday."

Outside the joint, a stereotyped horse's head, grotesque in its hugeness, wearing a horseshoe wreath of victory announced the place as The Paddock Bar and Grille. Across the street was the wide expanse of manicured lawn, vast acres of parking lot and the bulk of dark grandstands that comprised Santa Anita racetrack, quiet this early in the morning, but waiting for the flow of dedicated pony players. Here the horse followers could have the best of two worlds. Daytime races every summer and nighttime harness events under the lights.

On this side of the street, in the modest, low- roofed building housing The Paddock Bar and Grille, the players could have the best of two worlds, too, if they were in the know. The horseshoe-shaped, dark wooden bar was well stocked with every imaginable spirit, and the food was excellent. Some of the best available anywhere in the greater Los Angeles area. And they could enjoy off-track betting in the back. For years, The Paddock had been the legal front for Charlie Cavallera's illegal gambling operations. The large back office setup was located behind the convivial surroundings of the outer room.

Most of the race crowd would not be there until

around eleven, but the place was filled. A timid man, in off the streets, would have turned and left without a word. Like a deer, often the timid can sense the feral odor of the hunter. Today, the Paddock was filled with hunters. The two-legged creatures these hard-muscled, cold-eyed men made their game were those who had drawn fatal attention to themselves from the high-ranking echelon of la Cosa Nostra.

There was, plenty of subdued talk and lots of drinking, for this was a wake. For the second day in a row now, the small book operators, runners, button men, and street soldiers who acted as enforcers—all in fact, who comprised Charlie Cavallera's organization had gathered here to speculate on who would become Charlie's successor. They were here to swap rumors and gossip. Lack of direct supervision, because of his new assignment, had already taken a toll in efficiency and with Charlie's unexpected death the system had ground to a halt. That was costing the Family a lot of money and could not long be tolerated.

Seated among the others, near the center of the big horseshoe bar, was a powerful-looking, muscular individual. At first look, he appeared to be in superb condition, a finely tuned battling machine. But, on closer examination, one observed the white spiderweb lines of scars in the tanned flesh of jaw and cheekbones, the thickening of scar tissue around his eyebrows, prematurely graying hair and the vacant stare in his eyes and one realized they were looking at one of the world's losers.

"Hey, Louie! Lumpy Louie," the bartender called out as he made his rounds.

"Yeah, yeah," the loser responded to his name. "Whatcha doin' here?" pressed the barman. "Yeah, yeah I...I liked Mr. Cavallera. He was a nice man. Yeah, yeah. I wanted to show my res ...respek, you know?"

"Ya hear that?" growled a bearlike voice from Louie's right. "He wants to show his respect. Leave him be, Sid. Even a guy like him thought the Chief was great." The speaker turned to Lumpy Louie. "Have a beer on me, Louie."

"Yeah, yeah. Make it milk, though, huh Bear? I'm in trainin'. Gonna make a comeback, ya know. Some club fights, take on some of these wise-guy Mex comers. Yeah, yeah."

"Sure, Louie, sure," Bear Brollini replied, a note of sympathy entering his voice. "You'll slay 'em, man, you'll wipe 'em out." Even though he operated a small book in Charlie's regime and had been number-two muscle for the late Capo for many years, Bear Brollini had a sentimental side. There was a soft spot in his heart for those less fortunate than himself or those, like himself who could never qualify for the Mr. America contest. No one remembered Bear's first name. He was a classic example of his moniker; he had hardly any neck, broad shoulders, barrel-like middle, bulging legs and a thick pelt of black hair that covered his entire body and had been his curse since early adolescence. Add to that his basso profundo voice and the illusion was complete. Hey, Bear, who you think'll take

Charlie The Horse's place? asked a bookie down the bar.

"Nobody can 'take' his place, dummy," Brollini rumbled back. "Who you figure it'll be?"

"I got my money on Nate the Computer. That brain of his has everything stored in it better than one of them IBM machines, clicks out facts like hell won't have 'em."

"Feldman? Bullshit!" Bear roared back. "Hell, he ain't even Italian, let alone Sicci. They won't let no kike take control. I been about as Close to the Chief as anyone, but I ain't Sicci, so I ain't got a chance. Find yerself a new boy." Bear dismissed the idea with a wave of his pawlike hand. "I'll lay ya eight, five, or even, that the guy that's in there right now will be the new boss."

At that moment, the number-two man to Stan Ollivetti, "that guy in there now," entered through the light-and-sound-baffled doors separating the "Back Room" from The Paddock. He stood for a few seconds, surveying the assemblage of hoods, hustlers and hangers-on. In the true spirit of a wake, booze, bullshit and bon homme flowed freely. A little too freely from the looks of it. Everyone had a drink in front of him and-no one seemed in full control of himself. Then the trigger artist spotted Lumpy Louie and his glass of milk. He crossed to the bar in swift, measured strides, tapping the punchy ex-fighter on the shoulder.

"What's in that glass?" he demanded.

"Yeah, yeah. Milk, just milk."

"Okay, inside," jerking a thumb over his shoulder.

"Hey, Louie," an anonymous voice called in cruel jest, "ya finally got a break. You're gonna be our new boss!"

"Don't pay them bastards no mind, Louie. Just be straight with them and show respect, everything will be okay."

"Yeah, yeah. Tanks, Bear."

"Jeez! Scrapin' the bottom, aintcha?" Stan The Man groused when Lumpy Louie was brought before him. He was seated at the big desk from which Charlie Cavallera had ran his operation. A scowl darkened his face.

"He was the only one sober, boss. Other than Bear Brollini, and he wouldn't like being a messenger boy."

"So, we go wit Punchy here," Ollivetti snapped. "You know DeFalco Construction Company, Punchy?"

"Yeah, yeah. De one wit de whirlybirds?"

"That's it. How'd you know?"

"Mr. Cavallera, I got a lot of respek for Mr. Cavallera, sorry what happened to him, he was a good man. Mr. Cavallera, he sent me there, two, three times. Wit little envelopes like a Western Union boy."

"Okay, so you're gonna do it again, for me?" The Capo scribbled on a note pad and put the message into an envelope. "Take this and give it to the guy who runs the choppers...the, ah, whirlybirds. No one else, understand?" Ollivetti dug into his pocket, peeling a twenty off the wad in his money clip. "Take a taxi. Here's a double sawbuck to pay for it. Now get going."

Lumpy Louie stepped into the phone booth at the

edge of the large, crowded parking lot of The Paddock. He fumbled for the number and a dime. With a little difficulty, he dialed right the first time.

"Hello, Club Fighters, Limited. I'm sorry," the pleasant female voice murmured to Lumpy Louie, "there is no one in the office at this time. This is a recording. At the sound of the tone, if you will leave your name, number and any message, your call will be returned as soon as Mr. Hanson arrives. This is the tone..."

"Funny," the thought passed briefly through Lumpy Louie's mind, "every time I call there's no one there. But they did promise to book me some fights...and there are those bonuses they pay when I run an errand for Mr. Cavallera and tell them about it." Quickly he gave his message and called a cab.

MARK HARDIN HAD SPENT the day cleaning up a few small details in Long Beach and Inglewood. Now, before heading north to the San Bernardino Freeway and The Stronghold, nearly a hundred and forty miles distant, he stopped to check his dead-drop telephone number.

The telephone was located in Professor Haskins' townhouse apartment and was now listed under the Cover name William Hanson, Jr., a name that had served him well for an alternate identity and a verifiable place of employment and residence. It was attended twenty-four hours a day by an, answering device. Mark steadfastly refused to dial the regular number and listen to the pleasant-voiced woman on the other end. It was Donna Morgan's voice and Mark didn't feel ready yet to handle ghosts. He dialed the alternate number and triggered the playback with his tone pencil.

He stopped the playback after Lumpy Louie's message to digest the implications. For the first time the ex-fighter had identified DeFalco's outfit as "that place where the whirlybirds are." Mark was looking for the chopper involved in the heroin delivery. Had he found it that easily? It just might be. He opened his shirt and removed five twenties from, one compartment of his moneybelt, which contained $5,000 for emergency use, then located a Club Fighters, Ltd. envelope and letterhead. He scrawled a brief note and folded everything into the envelope, addressing it to Lumpy Louie at his skid row hotel. Now he was ready for any other messages.

"...must think I don't remember so well, so they talk right out in front, ya know?" Lumpy Louie's voice came again over the wire. "The word had come down that Mr. Cavallera's red bomb had been seen out on the desert, so they had two whirlybirds out lookin' around. I waited a long time, yeah, so I could take back some good news to Mr. Ollivetti, but they never came back. One guy did radio he thought he'd found somethin'. Yeah, yeah. So I come back. Thought you'd like to know even that little news, seein' as how I guess you'se is a good pal of Mr. Cavallera's too."

By all the angels in heaven and half the population

of hell! He might have found something! Two choppers in the desert to investigate? Images of slight, fragile-boned Willard Haskins in the hands of Mafia goons spurred Mark to action.

Driving his own car, a powerful Mazda RX-3 Sportster, Mark poured the coal to it. Weaving in and out of traffic, he was eating up the miles. He hoped, with slow-dying conviction, that he wouldn't arrive too late...

5

"LET THE DEAD"

SITTING UNDER COVER OF A LOW-BRANCHED COPSE of trees in a gully some five miles distant from The Stronghold, Mark Hardin was primed for action. Through the early morning hours, he had monitored the radio equipment in Charlie's Ferrari, eavesdropping on the deployment of two choppers and six cars full of hard men. Beside him, in the other seat, was another communications system, one connecting Professor Haskins, David Red Eagle and himself. Each set was equipped with a small black box—built by an electronics expert friend of Willard Haskins—that scrambled their messages and insured security. As he waited, the portable radio crackled and commanded his attention.

"There's one of them over the place now," Willard Haskins' voice came through tinnily. "Looks to be the same one as yesterday. Advise, over."

"Does he have a make on the place?" Mark queried.

"Can you locate him and get numbers without exposing yourself? Over."

"Can do, Mark. He can in no way see this place. I designed it that way. Will change locations and keep you advised. Out."

"Rog. Out," Mark snapped back automatically. As yet, there was no positive contact outside the area of The Stronghold. He leaned back and relaxed a few seconds.

His high-speed dash back to the desert on the previous evening had proven to be unnecessary. Apparently, Professor Haskins speculated, the helicopters had lost radio contact while crossing the San Bernardinos. It was a common thing to occur. True, they had hovered around the place for a while, but had at last gone on their way. The three men held a council of war. They decided to use this to advantage for another strike. They refrained from painting the Ferrari, setting it up as bait. Mark acquired some special equipment for the engagement and the radios were checked out. Then they all got a long night's sleep. David Red Eagle was first up and away, getting in position for the part he would eventually play in all of this. Before dawn, Mark was in position in his concealed spot.

"DFX-one, this is DFX-two. Bring up your chopper. I wanna get a closer look at that hill we was wonderin' about last night."

"Rog, DFX-two. Will bring in ground units. Out." As the chopper pilot switched frequencies, Mark snapped alert. "Ground one and two, this is air one.

Move to hard-surface road, off to left of highway one mile east your, present position. Turn left into same.

"Received, von Richtohfen. Say, just was thinkin'," the voice went on, "that bomb of Charlie's got a radio. If it's on this frequency, we better not use the radios. Over."

"How are we going to coordinate this mess? Over."

There was a long pause before a reply hit the air. "Yeah. That's right. We'll come up with somethin'. For now, let's just hope he's dumb. Coming up on the road now. Out."

Mark turned to his own radio find spoke quickly, "On their way, Professor. Looks like this is it. Let me know when you spot them."

"Make it now, my boy. Two cars and two helicopters."

"Time to saddle up the cavalry and ride to the rescue, then. I'll coordinate from here. Out."

"Luck, boy. Out."

Mark fired up the big mill in the Ferrari and fogged out of concealment, anting down the arroyo toward the highway. Tires spinning on loose gravel, he whipped onto the macadam surface and headed toward the turnoff. Off to his left he could see one of the choppers hovering closer to the road than to the distant mountain housing their hideout. Driving the speedometer above ninety-five, Mark flashed past the turnoff, heading further out onto the desert.

Above the action on the desert floor, Larry Novak saw the flash of red from the corner of his vision, hurtling past the road into the area they were concentrating on. He banked his chopper to verify what he thought he had seen. There was no doubt.

"Bingo! Hey, Musician," he radioed to Julio "Julie the Musician" Piccolo, leader of the headhunting crew in the lead car below. "Hey! We got the wrong place. Just spotted the red car tearing right past the turnoff. Going east at about a hundred.

"Gawdammit!" Julio swore. "Are you sure?"

"Hell yes, I'm sure. I seen it enough times from the air. That's Charlie's car."

"Then we got the wrong place?" The Musician was hot to find the gang responsible for this.

"Looks like it from here. Say, Musician, what about that radio in the car?"

"Hope he don't know about it, like I said. But I got another answer. Parlate 'taliano, capisce?"

"What about me?" Novak wanted to know.

"Lei paisan pro…aw, hell, give it to the guy next to you. He'll tell you what we're sayin'."

"Rog." He handed the mike to the hard man next to him. "Tell him I'm sendin' the other chopper back toward Barstow to keep an eye out for the fuzz. And tell him I'll only be giving position reports from now on."

MARK THROTTLED BACK on the big Ferrari mill, allowing the distance to close a little. He didn't want to lose his pursuers right yet. He chuckled as he heard Julie the Musician's instructions. "Ese biene," he said to himself. "Intellignente supreme lei Mafiosi." Five semesters of skull work at UCLA and that refresher course in Italian at the Army Language School were going to pay off.

Julio Piccolo was sure of a payoff on this one. No slob could escape a chopper. Shit, man, he was already counting the head money for bringing in this punk alive. If his pals—and he must have had a couple on that hit—weren't with him, they'd find out where they were soon enough. He grabbed the mike again and ordered the other cars into a roughly square search pattern, cutting off all hope of escape ahead or to either side. Licking his lips, Julie the Musician looked down the road at the tiny dot that was their quarry. The guy was braking; "Right in front of him!" came a cry in slurred Sicilian from the radio. "He's hit the brakes. Jesus. He's coming your way!"

Mark Hardin spotted the carload of button men coming toward him in the black Buick before they saw him. He hit the binders, nursing the wheel to allow the big machine to go into a rear-end drift, executing a controlled one-eighty. They had just reacted as he was well into his reversal of direction and downshifting, leadfooting it out of there. Freeing one hand, he snapped off three shots from the Colt Commander as he gained distance.

"Damn, that was close," he thought, his eyes looking frantically for a side road. He located one as Julie the Musician's staccato Italian syllables crackled from the radio.

"We're broadside in the road. I see him coming. No way he can get past us. Hang in there, Gunner, and we got this turkey sewed up." Julie and his boys hit the pavement behind their huge Continental, unlimbering their weapons.

"Will ya look at that," one of the hard men exclaimed, admiration clear in his voice.

In front of their improvised roadblock, Mark Hardin had swung the Ferrari into a tire-punishing, head-snapping ninety-degree turn, taking to a narrow dirt road leading away from the expected ambush. He grasped the wheel and poured on more speed. As a rooster-tail of dust fogged out behind, Mark searched his mental map for a connecting road that would lead him back to the main highway. As he thought, he picked up the mike to the Command II and advised his cohorts, "I figure we have about five minutes now. They're pretty slow getting under way behind and so far no more cars in front. Check in again later."

They were a little slow getting on Mark's trail because the Buick load of hard men nearly slammed into Julio's crew wagon as it followed the unexpected racing turn executed by the Ferrari. By the time they were unscrambled and under way, Mark had gained an impressive lead.

Julie the Musician was boiling now. The wise-ass punk in that car was a real wheel man, no denying, but enough was enough. He grabbed the mike again. "Cars four and six, move in. He's on a crossroad between us. Three and five, move onto the highway.

Go east. No, make it one each way. We gotta get this bastard!"

High above them, Larry Novak caught another turn by the red car. He nudged the Mafioso next to him. "Tell yer boss he's headed west now. Have car six come up another mile and tum in and he should cut him off."'

After the instructions were relayed, the pilot watched with growing excitement as the cars converged on a single spot, like pieces in a chess game when an opponent's weak spot is finally found. Far out ahead of the others, one crew wagon and the red streak of the Ferrari were on a collision course and, if their estimated speeds were correct, they would hit any second now. Both cars careened into the intersection of two dirt roads. Then something went wrong, very wrong indeed.

Mark saw the approaching crew buggy and made a dive for the canvas bag on the floorboards beside him. He found what he wanted by feel and pulled it out, jerking the pin and slipping the spoon. Transferring it to his left hand, he counted off the seconds, then lobbed it through the open right-hand window of the head party's car as it closed on his fender, less than four feet away. He swerved hard right onto the other road, heading toward the highway again. Behind him, the grenade went off inside the car, scattering bits and pieces of glass, steel, bodies and igniting gasoline. It sent up an ugly red and black bloom into the clear desert air. One down!

Mark covered the mile to the highway in forty seconds. Braking hard, he headed again to the east. Over the radio, he heard anger, frustration and new orders from his pursuers. He smiled to himself and lengthened his lead. His eyes searched out the one particular road he was heading for as he continued to burn time.

"He's turning off again. Heading down a road toward a cluster of hills. That must be his hiding place."

"Which road, which road?" Julie demanded angrily.

"Two miles ahead of you. Good news. There's no other roads going off it. He's trapped himself. You got the only way in."

Things suddenly looked better for Julie the Musician. A trap. Damn well deserved it. Taking but a whole carload of boys like that. What the hell did he use? He shouted orders into the mike, but had to slow down, calm his voice and repeat that all cars were to come to the highway and follow him down this new road.

"I'm above the hills," came the voice from their radio. There's a box canyon-like area here. He seems to be heading toward it."

"We gottcha!" Julie crowed. Box canyon. Just like them Western flicks on TV. Cut 'em off at the pass. Show that dumb bastard.

Another message came in, worried. "Uh-ooh. Looks like this isn't the road he wants. He's stopped. Tryin' to turn around. He can see it's a dead end."

"Pour it on, ya slob," Julie demanded of his driver. "We got the bastard, we got him now!"

Just as the big Continental turned off the highway, another message came over the radio. "He's given up, he's pullin' on into the canyon."

"Down!" Julie ordered the chopper pilot. "Get down there and plug that hole. We're on the way in. We sure got his ass now. Get it down and we'll back you up in a few minutes."

Jouncing onto the rough dirt track, the four remaining cars of the headhunting party followed their leader toward what was a certain capture. There was no escape for the punk in that Ferrari now. Engines whined as they sped along the rough ground. Three short miles and they passed the chopper; one car remained there to block off the narrow entrance to the canyon. The other cars braked to a halt beside that of their leader.

Julie the Musician stood beside his car, confused. He and his men were ready for a battle, but none came. The others piled from their cars and joined him. There was a sudden silence over the entire canyon. Ahead of them was Charlie's red Ferrari, doors open, motor silent. But nowhere could they see the driver, whom they had chased for a frantic fifteen minutes. No sound betrayed his presence.

Pop! Shussssh! From behind them came the unmistakable sound of a tire being punctured. They whirled in time to see a second and a third tire of the rear-guard car get hit by arrows! Before anyone could react, more arrows thudded into the bodies of the rear guard. They fell where they stood. One man gave a strangled cry as his throat was pierced by a steel-barbed shaft.

"Spread out, you guys!" Julie commanded, sending his men scattering among the rocks.

Five of the button men standing beside the crew wagons, slow to obey the order, were the first to discover that there were new rules in this game. Slightly louder pops were followed by agonizing screams as scalding a pee of white phosphorous rained down on them. More pops, among the rocks, located the points where a steady rain of the deadly chemical bursts were going off. Men went down, screaming and writhing, all over the floor of the "sure thing trap" their leader had so enthusiastically described to them.

High up in the rocks, Mark Hardin continued to hurl the smooth, pale, blue green eggs down onto his would-be captors. When the supply was exhausted, he settled himself in a notch between two big boulders and sighted in with his big .44 Magnum. His first shot caught one hard man as he tried to dash from one boulder to another. He sprawled face first in the sandy soil, dead before he could feel it. The second silenced a screaming victim of the white phosphorous. Another and another shot thundered and rolled off the steep walls of the canyon. After the fifth shot, Mark changed to one of his special ten-round box magazines and continued his deadly work.

In less than three minutes—although to those spattered by the unquenchable hell of the phosphorous it seemed an eternity—not a man moved below. Mark checked the loads in his carbine, policed his expended brass and grenade safety rings, then broke cover, walking slowly down the slope at the end of the canyon. As he proceeded toward the cars, he examined each gunman, making sure he was dead. One twitching, groaning remnant of a human being was dispatched with a hip shot from the big Magnum. He moved on.

A slight movement caught at the edge of Mark's peripheral vision. He spun in his tracks, the deadly muzzle of his big blaster zeroing in as a form appeared among the rocks.

"Hey, hold it man. Hold it!" Julie the Musician whined. "That stuff you used, Jeez, it hurts! Don't blast me, man. I'm hurt. Real hurt."

"You the crew chief?" Mark's voice was fire and ice.

"Yeah. Julio Piccolo. Christ, you sure mousetrapped us. What is this?" He extended an arm, cloth from his jacket smoldering around a raw and angry wound that bubbled fiercely with a sickening stench of burning flesh. "It's...it's still burning in there."

Mark made sure the Mafioso was disarmed and seated with his feet tied before attending to the wound. Some of these swaggering hoods were really tough, he thought as he pried the small dot of burning chemical from the wound with his Buck clasp knife, and this Julie the Musician was one of fire genuine tough guys. Not one indication of pain escaped him during the operation.

Outside the canyon, at the first sounds of gunfire, Larry Novak, always cautious of the safety of his aircraft, started to lift his ungainly bird off the ground. As the rotors caught air and began to lift, the Mafioso beside him gave a soft grunt and fell away, his throat cut from ear to ear. In his place, suddenly, was the dark, grinning face of an old Indian.

"Sonofabitch!" the pilot gasped. .

"Don't fly," was the only command David Red Eagle gave the pilot. Pressing the bloodstained point of his knife into the flesh of Larry Novak's neck brought instant obedience. When the bird died, Red Eagle herded his prisoner before him, toward the scene of slaughter, where Mark now tended to Julie the Musician's wounds.

"Well, well," Mark remarked unnecessarily, as his Indian cohort, brought the pilot up to him. "We caught us a birdman." He looked from one prisoner to the other. They surveyed the dead men around them and cast anxious glances at the grim young man; who had defeated them.

"For starters," Mark addressed Larry Novak, "I'm going to make you an offer you just can't refuse."

"Don't give this son of a bitch nothin'," Julie the Musician shouted, recovering a little from the shock of the fire bomb attack and what followed.

"Damn it, Julie. You didn't do so fuckin' good," Novak snapped back.

Good. We can do business, Mark thought. Aloud, he told Novak, "I'm giving you a choice. You don't look like you qualify as a blood brother under the Omerta oath, You're one of the sheep, not a goat. Right?" The pilot nodded agreement. "So, you've little to lose. Work for me or join them," Mark's eyes compelled Larry Novak's eyes to turn and encompass the ghastly remains of the ambush victims.

"Name's Novak, mister," Larry Novak replied for answer, extending his hand. "I'm a damn good pilot, chopper mechanic, too. Glad to join up."

"Not yet," came Mark's retort. "You know what it will mean, joining me? You'll never be able to show your face where this one's paisans can find you. They'd snuff you on sight. And there's the possible problem of the law. I haven't exactly found out if there is a hood hunting license, so I might be in a lot of hot water over this."

"Hell with that. A live fugitive is a whole lot better than a dead—but Loyal—member of the organization. Count me in, Mister?"

"Later with the names. For you," he turned to the other prisoner, "I have something special. First a little question and answer game, then..." Mark's smile reminded Julio Piccolo of a shark he'd once seen. All teeth and no warmth. "Well, let's get to the questions."

"Go fuck yours—" Julie never completed the obscenity. Mark's big hand clapped him against his left ear, knocking him over on his injured arm. For the first time a scream tore from his lips.

"That's just my openers. Who set up this heroin operation Cavallera was involved in?"

Gasping back the pain, Julie worked his lips until

his mouth was moist enough, then he spat in Mark's face. Mark rocked back on his heels, wiping the spittle from his face and neck. Slowly and deliberately, he took Julie's arm in his hands and dug a thumb into the wound.

The gangster screamed again and again, went dead white and passed out. He revived to the odor of wood smoke, the acrid aroma of burning desert vegetation. Slowly he lifted himself and looked around. Mark was standing some distance from him, talking with the pilot. Off to the other side crouched the old Indian who had brought in Novak. He was slowly feeding small sticks to a nearly smokeless fire.

Carefully straining his hearing, Julie the Musician caught some of the soft words of their conversation.

"Hell, Mr. Hardin, I suppose you're right. Until it all broke in the paper, I didn't know it was heroin I was haulin' around. Thought it was something to do with Charlie's bookie operation. I'd done stuff like that before. That's how I learned my second paycheck came from the Syndicate. But drugs is somethin' else again. So, I fly for you as your chopper pilot. I got nothin' to lose and your money sounds a little cleaner."

Julie the Musician groaned aloud. The big guy who had shot them up started across the ground toward him. He couldn't help it, the groan, but at least he had a name. If he lived through this, Don Pietro would know what to do with that.

"Let's continue the questions," Mark said. "Who set

up the heroin deal for Charlie the Horse? Who's the supplier? Let's hear it all."

"Nothin'," Julie mumbled. His attention was taken by the fire that Red Eagle was tending. "What' he doin'? He gonna eat right here?" The idea sickened him.

"Oh, haven't you ever seen any Western flicks? It's an old Apache trick. He'll make small coals and put them on your belly, slowly burning a hole right through, you... That is if you don't answer my questions. Now, who set this deal up?"

"Kiss my ass," Julie replied.

Mark grasped his hair and pulled Julie's head back and around, giving him a full view of a grinning David Red Eagle, scooping up coals. "'Nother thing he might do. He'll build a small, slow fire between your legs, right up close. Just coals at first, then small twigs and then bigger until it roasts your prick right off..." He jerked Julie's head around again, throwing his captive's frightened eyes downward toward his groin. "And," Mark continued, "bursts your balls like popcorn..."

Julie the Musician, leading triggerman of the toughest (and deadest) head party in Southern California, talked. He told them everything he knew. Just to make sure, Mark Hardin took him through it all a second time.

"And this 'His Lordship,' you told about. Any idea who he might be?"

"I told ya. No. I...I would guess he might be some high-class English dude. You know, maybe with some embassy. Don Pietro keeps going on about immunity.

Must be that dipple…diplomatic immunity these foreigners got, right?"

"And you. Where do you fit in?"

"I took over temporary for Charlie, after you hit him."

Mark placed the muzzle of his Colt Commander between Julio's eyes, slowly clicking off the safety. The hood began to sweat. "That's the last lie you tell, Julie. We both know Stan the Man Ollivetti took over for Charlie. He's sitting in the 'back office' at The Paddock right now, giving the orders. Once more, what's your part in all this?"

Julio Piccolo wet his lips with a rapidly drying tongue, his eyes darting nervously from the big gun to the hard face of the man questioning him. "Don Pietro put me in charge of the crew that was supposed to take care of you." He shuddered slightly, licked his lips again. "Christ! You're a one-man army."

Mark replaced the pistol in his waistband. "No, not an army, my friend. Just a penetration team. I'm just a penetrator. If I had an army, I'd clean out all you scum in less than forty-eight hours.

"Now I have a message I want you to take to Don Pietro," Mark continued as he untied the gunsel's feet. "Tell 'em I'm coming after him. Tell him as long as he keeps on dealing drugs I'll come after him until there's no one left between him and me and then...then I'll make him die a long, slow death. You got that, Julie?"

"Yeah. Sure, sure," relief at the sudden reprieve overwhelmed Julie the Musician.

"Fine, Julie, fine. Now, let's get out of here." "What about these?" David Red Eagle asked; the first words he had spoken since taking the chopper.

Mark looked around at the sprawled corpses. "Let the dead bury their dead."

Burdened by an extra passenger, the helicopter skimmed the ground on the way from the box-canyon ambush. Mark retrieved his Ferrari and drove it out to the highway. About a mile from the main road, the chopper lowered to eight feet above the ground.

"Remember what you were told to tell your boss," Red Eagle said as he opened the door of the bubble canopy. "Highway is one mile that way," he pointed as he pushed the speechless Mafioso out of the helicopter.

Below, Mark's car reached the macadam and both vehicles headed by random route to The Stronghold. Already, Mark's mind was sifting through the details, planning the next move.

6

IMPORTANT CONFERENCES

"Trot that one past me again, Musician," Don Pietro commanded his chief enforcer. "Just how in hell did you go out there, lose thirty-six guys, a helicopter and its pilot, and still be alive to come back and tell me about it?"

Julio Piccolo was sweating, sweating more than he had done under the icy gaze of Mark Hardin. He stood before Don Pietro Scarelli's desk flanked by Tutti and Frutti Gambini, twin gunsels working for Stan Ollivetti. He wasn't on trial, exactly, but he was certainly under a very dark cloud of distrust. Unconsciously, he wiped at the beads of moisture on his forehead. "Look, Don Pietro, he...he saved me. Like a messenger, like. He shot up the others, God! I know he could see me from where he was, but he didn't shoot at me. Then he comes down, straight to where I was, calm as can be and cuts this phosphorous outta me."

"And you didn't pop him then!" screamed the Don.

Julie the Musician cringed from the anger of his master. "You never had this stuff burnin' inside you. I tell ya, it'll bring ya to your knees. I peed my pants. And not ashamed to admit it. Nothin' ya can do stops it. It takes all yer strength. I couldn't even hold up my rod."

"Shit!" Don Pietro drank from his ever-present ice water and glowered at his once-top rodman. "So what's this message he gave you for me?"

"Well—you ain't gonna like this, Don Pietro—he says to me, he says: 'Tell him I'm coming after him. Tell him as long as he keeps on dealing drugs I'll come after him until there's no one left between him and me and then...'"

"Enough!" Don Pietro nodded to the twins and they departed. Julie heaved a silent sigh of relief. At least the heat was off him for a minute or so. "Stan, you hear that?" asked the old Mafioso. "This punk...ah, what's his name?"

"Hardin," Julie provided, happy to be included in as an almost equal again.

"This Hardin punk says he's comin' after me. Hell, before dumb-dumb here spilled his guts, he didn't even know my name. Now he sends his tame pussycat runner here with a message he's comin' after me. Basta! Pussycat runners we don't need. Guys called Hardin we don't need. You put pussycat here on ice until you can get a real handle on this Hardin punk, then...then we make a big object lesson of them both...somethin' everybody can look at and know they don't screw with this Family."

Sudden realization that his reprieve was no reprieve at all turned Julio Piccolo's bowels to ice water. "Oh no!" he moaned aloud. "Oh, sweet Christ, no. Please, Don Pietro. You gotta understand, I didn't have a choice. I didn't have no chance. Please understand."

"I understand one thing. You cost me damn near every button man I got—Hell, I gotta call guys up from San Diego, hustle outside talent from Vegas and you want another chance. Just to keep control of my territory; I might even have to go through that guy in Montreal for some Moustache Petes from the old country to cover for the guys you got wiped out there. Shit, Musician, I'll give you your chance right here and now if you want to die fast."

Julie the Musician hadn't cried since he was six, but big tears rolled down his face, his hands shook and his eyes were wild with fear. "No, Don Pietro. Please give me another chance. It wasn't my fault!" The old Don made a small gesture with his hand.

A sign as old as the brotherhood, surviving even the journey to this country. As he continued to hold Julie's attention, Stan Ollivetti took his .380 Beretta from its shoulder rig, screwed the six-inch silencer onto its muzzle and stepped behind the unlucky triggerman.

Julie was going on, extolling his respect for the Don, his status as a father and a Family man when the slug caught him at the base of his head, tracking upward. His eyes bugged and blood began to run from his ears. The light, underpowered .380 slug didn't break out of his skull, but it did push up a bulge that wasn't there before. Julie the Musician Piccolo had played his last notes in the Mafia serenade. He slumped forward in his chair and fell lifeless to the floor.

"Get rid of that garbage," Don Pietro commanded.

"Yes, sir, Don Pietro," Stan the Man replied, returning his silenced piece to its leather. "Now, this Hardin. With only a last name, we're gonna have it rough finding him. Guy comes on this hard; odds are you won't find him in the phone book. Not even all five phone books for LA."

"I know that," came the Don's short reply. "We got ways. Just you see you use them. Everything secure for the next pickup?"

"Yes, sir. But, ah...Don Pietro?"

"Yes, Stan? Problems?"

"That pilot. This Novak character. He was supposed to fly in the contact. He knows about the meet."

"Even better. There's where we shall have our Mister Smart-ass Hardin. See to it."

"This I like even better and better," Stan the Man commented as he summoned his twin gunmen to haul out the remains of Julio Piccolo. "Only one thing, Don Pietro. We can have no more than three guys at the pickup. How we take him with three, when he just knocked over thirty-six?"

"Those boys'll be in from Diego tonight. Set 'em up at your hard site and fill them in on the situation. We can only send three but, but this guy has to come in and out to make the hit, right? So nothin' says we can't have all approaches covered on the way in and out, got it? We'll get us a fine Mr. Hardin this time."

Chief Deputy Sheriff Paul Harris was fielding the questions following a statement made by Sergeant Kelly Patterson. He was doing a good job of it, too, until one reporter threw him a vicious curve. "Is it true we have a full-scale gangland war on our hands, Paul?"

"Not that we are aware of," came his bland reply.

"Then what accounts for the thirty-six hoods that were killed early this morning over near Barstow?"

It caught the Chief Deputy off guard, but he recovered quickly. "That's news to me. Besides, that happened in San Bernardino County. Nothing to connect it to the case we're discussing."

"From what I hear," persisted the reporter, "they were all on Don Pietro Scarelli's payroll. Wouldn't that make it your concern?"

"If what you say is true. But, first of all, you must realize that Peter Scarelli is a reputable businessman. Unless and until we have positive proof to the contrary, I cannot give official sanction to press rumors or publicly state that he has any connection with organized crime." They laughed on cue and Harris went on. "As I said, if this report of yours is true, we will have to give it careful thought and study before releasing anything to the press." Whatever the reporter's source, it was faster than official channels. Before the Chief Deputy could continue, a message was handed to him. He read it, blanched, and crumpled the paper. "I'm sorry, gentlemen. Urgent business causes me to end this press conference. Thank you all. You have printed copies of the official text. Good afternoon."

"Have anything to do with the gang war, Chief?" called the knowledgeable reporter as they broke up.

Back in his office, Paul Harris called for Kelly Patterson. When the younger detective was seated, he handed him the crumpled note. Kelly read it and whistled tunelessly.

"I'll be damned," he replied. "Sure does look like this is connected to our Cavallera killing. But, cripes, who in hell's doing it? White phosphorous for God's sake. That sounds like the army. What I want to know is how one guy, even with those hell-bombs, can take out thirty-six hoods and apparently not even get a scratch." He looked up as two men entered the office. George Hart and Shaun. Thomas. The latter grinned broadly and winked at Kelly.

"I thought I'd learn a little more if I hung around. What is this, a gathering of the clan?"

Chief Deputy Harris started to growl at the reporter, but Kelly waved him back to his chair. "Relax, Paul. Shaun's a tame one. He won't break anything until we tell him it's okay. Hi, George. You people come to the same conclusion we did?"

"More or less, Kelly. But I'm afraid this shoots down your one-man theory."

"Why's that?" Kelly's confidence in his pet theory was hard to destroy. Beside him, Shaun Thomas leaned forward, expectantly, but careful from past experience not to disturb the fine balance that allowed him to witness this scene.

"We have a full report from San Bernardino on this mess. Tire tracks from Michelin Radials—so that Ferrari may well have been used by the same man—lot of guys shot full of forty-four slugs. So far, you might be right, but..."

"Cut the mystery-story bit, George," Kelly urged.

"Four guys had arrows sticking out of them."

"Arrows!" both of the Sheriff's men chorused. "Yeah. Tires on one crew wagon shot out with arrows, too. The arrows were shot from behind, the slugs from the front. So, simply impossible to be one guy alone, you agree?"

"Kee-aich-rist!" Kelly bellowed. "First it's the army chuckin' willie peter at the Mafia and now comes the Indians. Sure the Seventh Cavalry ain't in there somewhere, George?"

"Maybe closer than you think. One of our experts in ethnology, happens to be attached to this office, identified the arrows as authentic Cheyenne. Real Indian arrows, made the old-fashioned way, like they did a hundred years ago. Figure that one out, you Irish wiseacre."

They all sat in silence for a moment. At last, unable to contain himself, Shaun broke into their thoughts. "Okay, so let me get this straight. So far we have some guy with access to the nearest army arsenal throwing white phosphorous bombs at the hoods and a hundred-year-old Indian knocking them over with a bow and arrows? Bullshit! It just don't wash. Even for the 'Late-Late Show.' Even for my paper it don't wash. You're FBI, right?" he addressed his question to George Hart. "Come on, fella, give. What's the real story?"

Grinning at the reporters' inability to grasp that they were deadly serious, George made short reply. "You have it right there. Nothing more, nothing less."

"At least it leaves us one possibility," Kelly interposed. "Paul, you remember that auto accident—what was it; three, four, five weeks ago? Up near Big Bear? Some guy called it in to the substation up there. Wouldn't give his name or anything. Said the car was run off the road by hoods working for Charlie Cavallera. A girl was killed in it."

"Right," Paul replied. "I seem to remember she was related to somebody...ah, a Doctor Willard Haskins, right?"

"That's the one. His niece. He's retired now, but he used to teach at USC, a real police buff. Always ready to bang your ear over his theories of how to end organized crime. Could be?"

"An old guy like that," Paul dismissed it. "Hell, he's in his late sixties. Forget it."

"Let me finish, Paul. We did a routine check; after all there was a death involved. She was dating a guy named Hardin, Mark Hardin. He never showed up anywhere, so we figured he died in the accident. We conducted a wide search, but you know those mountains. The body, or at least the bones could turn up any time, even years from now. No signs of foul play, so we wrote it off as two killed. But that still leaves our Professor Haskins. He has a townhouse apartment and a place in the desert. In the Calico Mountains near Barstow. Making more sense?"

"Not to me, you're not," Shaun said, standing up. "Cowboys and Indians was bad enough, now you bring in Mad Professors. Don't worry about a press leak, gentlemen. If I even tried to get this published, my boss would have me on the way to the funny farm faster than you could pull the pin on one of those phosphorous grenades you're yellin' about. Good-bye and good luck."

7
WSRD

"YOU KNOW," MARK COMMENTED AS HE LAID DOWN the piece of steel tubing he was working with, "there's a special outfit in the Pentagon—I swear it's true—that's called the Department of Obfuscation. Their job is to make sure everything has a bureaucratic name, nothing simple permitted, it has to be confusing. They'd call this," referring to the work he and Professor Haskins were engaged in, "Weapons Systems Research and Development."

Willard Haskins was examining what appeared to be a child's plastic water pistol: With small jewelers' tools, he was making minute adjustments of its internal parts. He declined comment on Mark's rambling patter. Rather, satisfied with his efforts, he reassembled the plastic weapon and sighted on a straw target near at hand. The strange device hissed softly and the professor was rewarded with a solid, smacking noise from the target. "Low and left," he said offhand.

"What?" Mark inquired. "Are you still working with that toy?"

"This 'toy,' as you call it, my boy," came the older man's reply, "is a highly precise piece of work, done for me by one of the foremost ballistics fabricators in the country. Never disparage that which is new or unconventional. Once this little gem is refined, it just may save your life or someone else's someday."

"Yeah, if it works, and if the dosage problem can be worked out, and if a plastic gas cylinder doesn't leak before it's needed. Me?" Mark walked across the workroom floor to a bench where a foot-long piece of quarter-inch dowling was clamped in a vice. "I prefer this method. Swift, sure and silent."

He began to wrap a six-inch-wide strip of brass screen around the dowel. The first several layers were carefully tied to prevent them from unrolling. Then his work progressed faster, until the strip of brass wire, twelve-feet long, was condensed into a roll that would slip inside the steel tubing which Mark had been working on moments before. Professor Haskins did not deign to reply to such poorly thought out criticisms of his project, so Mark continued to work in silence.

Using the excellent equipment in the professor's workroom, he silver soldered a second metal-sided rubber washer into place, sealing the roll of screen inside the tube. A few quick strokes with a file and the L-shaped key slot in the other end of the tube was smoothed. From the workbench, Mark took a .22 high-standard trophy model target pistol. He attached the long cylinder to the muzzle, securing it to the barrel by locking it around the front sight post. He inserted a magazine of ten rounds and took aim at the straw dummy. For the first seven rounds, the loudest sound was the clack of metal on metal as the slide operated on the autoloading pistol. It was accompanied by a soft pfutting sound, as each forty-grain slug exited from the homemade silencer. The last three shots were louder, yet still far removed from anything a person could identify as a gunshot. Mark smiled in satisfaction.

"One more to make for the Ruger carbine and I'm finished for the day."

"I can understand your desire to change tactics, to use silent weapons, my boy, but a silencer greatly decreases the range. It seems you are eliminating the noise factor only to create another problem in its place."

Mark grinned ruefully. "I have a feeling I'm going to work much, closer to my target from now on, Professor. No, much as I like 'old reliable,' that forty-four Mag is just too noisy. We have the initiative now. The only way to keep it is to keep on hitting them where it hurts...and it hurts most in the pocketbook. So we take this next heroin shipment. And for that we need silence."

"Just how do you propose to handle this next strike?"

"Well, if you're through with your games, we'll hold a strategy conference."

"Games indeed," Willard Haskins muttered at Mark's broad back.

"You two are sure huffy lately. What you need is a

night out on the town. I thought David would pop a blood vessel over that crossbow. Said it was a downright sacrilege to produce a bow you shot from the shoulder. But, at least he's building a useful weapon. He should be back by now, shouldn't he?"

"Fine state of affairs, when the patient becomes the doctor. Yes, I believe he is back. And for your information, my toy is ready for a field test. I'll bring it along."

Half an hour later found all four members of the team gathered in the large living room of The Stronghold. Drinks in hand, they sat together, near the gigantic picture window. They were intently observing the body of a coyote; lying before them on the desert floor. When they had first come upstairs, Professor Haskins led them outside, where he released the coyote from a cage, shooting it with a small dart from the plastic pistol. It had continued to run a few steps, then it seemed to lose control of its muscles. It had wavered, fallen and thrashed about a bit on the ground. Then it lay still.

"As you know," Mark began, drawing their attention inside, "Larry here told us that the next shipment would be two days from now, at midnight. The location is the parking lot of a Family-owned warehouse in the City of Commerce. I just checked the phone drop and learned that they plan to play it clever and ambush me on the way in or out. No other change in plan. They've got you," he nodded toward Novak, "pegged as helping me now and figure you to give me the location. That means the Musician told everything. Fine. With the silent weapons, we're going to be ready for anything they have in mind."

"Ah, Marcus my boy," Willard Haskins interrupted. "If you will observe..." Everyone looked outside, where the coyote, which to all outward appearances had been dead, was slowly beginning to move around. Feebly, it was trying to get to its feet. "I used a very light dosage. Adequate for the demonstration, but quite dramatic in effect, no?"

"Ya made a damn fool of me," Larry Novak declared. "I never believed it would work."

"Make that double for me," Mark said. "Professor, I'm afraid I underestimated you. That thing just might have some very practical applications someday."

Professor Haskins produced one of the darts. It was nearly half an inch in diameter, some two and a quarter inches long. Thin metal fins recessed on springs into the shaft. A wicked-looking needle-sharp point protruded a half-inch beyond the body of the dart. "I have filled some with curarine in case you need to use them against the enemy, but the main idea was to solve the dilemma of what to do with innocent bystanders who wander into the line of fire. This isn't ready yet," he said, hefting the nonmetallic weapon, "for unrestricted use, but I have every confidence now that it has the potential for being the most formidable weapon in your arsenal."

Larry Novak spoke for them all, "If you could put a man away like you did that coyote, and then have him walk away like that, it'd be a real arguing point with the fuzz when it came to making the final body count."

Mark returned them to their original topic. "In light of their plans, I think it is time to present them with a very troublesome surprise."

David Red Eagle crossed to the television set, turning it on. As it warmed up, he commented, "As for surprises, you are going to be the feature item on the, noon news." No one was certain how Red Eagle came by these bits of information, but his unknown source had as yet to be proven inaccurate. The picture came into focus and Red Eagle turned up the volume.

"The day of The Godfather is supposedly ended and the voice of 'Our Thing' is no longer heard in the land. Or at least that is what some people prefer to believe. Yet, during this past week, a series of incidents in Los Angeles has captured the attention of the nation. Let's go now to Roger Philliphant, News Director of our network affiliate, KLAX-TV, in Los Angeles for this noon report."

Another image replaced that of the staid, reliably conservative anchorman of the Eastern news bureau. It was a much younger man sporting modish hairstyle and brush moustache above a "California informal" Edwardian suit, wide, high-collared pastel shirt and wildly colored, ample tie. He smiled disarmingly into the lens and began his spiel.

"The days of Bugs Moran and the Saint Valentine's Day Massacre have long passed. Yet during the past six days, gangland warfare—complete with blazing tommy-guns, exploding automobiles and violent death—has returned to Southern California. Within a radius of two-hundred miles from the Police Building, on the steps of which I am now standing, thirty-eight men have died—some of them most horribly." He held up a pale blue-green, egg-shaped metal canister, not much larger than a small orange. It had a light yellow band around its wider middle. "Twenty-five of these men were victims of a deadly chemical, white phosphorous, used almost exclusively by the military. An unbelievable assortment of knives, arrows and guns dispatched the others. Although the reputations of these men were unsavory, their connection, if any, to organized crime or a syndicate has yet to be proved.

"At the time of this report, neither the District Attorney's office nor the Sheriff's Department has released any statement regarding the possible identity of the persons responsible for these slayings. The first to die in this recent fracas was the known Mafia figure, Charlie the Horse Cavallera, which brings speculation that the killings are the result of internecine warfare. In light of this, serious consideration is being given to a request for Federal assistance.

"This is Roger Philliphant, KLAX-TV, Los Angeles."

The slightly graying anchorman replaced him in a-slow dissolve. 'The sounds of gunfire in Los Angeles have not gone unheard on Capitol Hill. Here, by videotape recording is the text of an announcement made by Senator Martyn Corvus, chairman of the Senate Permanent Subcommittee on Crime and Violence, released at noon today, Eastern Standard Time."

A long, slow dissolve replaced the clock-studded

wall of the New York network office with the steps of the New Senate Office Building in Washington, D.C.

Standing on the steps was the familiar, distinguished figure of Martyn Corvus. His square-jawed, gray-eyed face was drawn into deep lines of worry and concern. "My fellow Americans," came the rich baritone voice that some said was that of the next President of the United States, "the seriousness of the incidents now occurring in Los Angeles has been apparent to my committee. That there exists a real possibility of open gang warfare in Southern California is a subject for sober consideration. Therefore, we have decided to send investigators to Los Angeles to determine the extent, if any, of violation of Federal statutes and the possibility of intervention by Federal authorities. It is my hope that this violence shall not continue. But, should it do so, I pledge to you that my committee shall do its utmost to insure the return of safety to your city streets and an end to unbridled violence.

"The criminal mind cannot conceive of rights for any but their own kind. We stand steadfast behind a return to law and order and—as a committee—shall do all in our power to encourage and assist local law enforcement in ending this assault on the peace and safety of the City of Angels."

His stocky body, with its stem face, was quickly replaced by a map of the lower Mississippi River. Off camera, the voice of the News Director continued; "Senator Corvus also indicated that he was going to give this situation close, personal attention. Elsewhere, rapid repair of the unexpectedly collapsed dikes has caused flood waters to recede from the banks of the Missis..."

Red Eagle turned off the television. Only a slight twinkle in his eyes betrayed his inner feelings. "You are becoming as my friend the Wind Walker, striking everywhere but seen nowhere. It is good. As he brought terror to the White Hood cross burners, so shall you to the Black Hand." Suddenly a smile creased his lined old face. Nodding to the glass in Mark's hand, he said, "You may have two tonight. You have done well."

Darkness had come to the desert. The immensity of the bright, hard light of myriad stars was even more awe-inspiring than the glitter of nighttime Los Angeles. Two men stood outside The Stronghold, enjoying the evening coolness.

In a voice made small by the greatness of the vista around them, Larry Novak spoke. "Tell me—you never did, you know—" he added parenthetically, "why you began this vendetta?"

Mark Hardin took a deep breath, savoring the cool, scented air, taking time to think, to organize his many reasons into one sensible, intelligent argument in support of his quixotic crusade, with its trail "of blood and death. He let the breath rush out of him in a sustained sigh.

"There was a girl, Donna Morgan," he began. "The Professor's niece. She was young, pretty, full of life and curiosity. She...she helped bring me back from a pretty low point in my life. Through her, I found my family and my heritage—I don't know if that means anything to you or not? She set me on the right road."

"I know," the chopper pilot replied. "For me, her name was Nakamura Ichi…she died in childbirth. He would have been my son…"

"Anyway, after we had looked into my past, learned who Mark Hardin was, where he had come from, we went on to find other things. We found each other, fell in love I suppose you could say.

"Then we got involved in discovering who the guy was who was responsible for my back getting mangled the first time. Learning what happened to him became important. That led to organized gambling and that brought us to Charlie The Horse. Never did find out about Rammer."

"Rammer?" interrupted Larry Novak. "Seems I've heard that name around."

"Yeah. Rammer Norton. Played for UCLA when I was there. He also played footsie with the Mafia."

"Hey! I do know him. At least the name. Not around LA now, as far as I know. But his name's come up among some of the guys before. He's still connected, all right. He's top-level muscle—college grad and all that shit, very smooth, but mean as hell."

"Time for him later. Anyway, Donna and I got onto this heroin thing—just the edge of it—but enough to get real interested. Something slipped, leaked out. They came after us. Ran our car off the road. Donna was trapped inside. She burned to death…and the accident left me just about as busted up as I was when I got back from 'Nam."

"Christ," Novak said softly.

"As I started healing, I made a vow to get them. Get a hundred for Donna and another hundred, maybe, for me. Nothing else mattered during all the weeks I was recovering. We—the three of us—made a pact. Willard—the Professor—and David Red Eagle came up with more cash than I believed possible. Set up a cover identity for me, an apartment in town, a car amid everything necessary to let me disappear, then infiltrate the mob's operation.

"Of course they had their own, private motives for helping me do what we've done, for going as far as we have. So have I. It's become more than just simple vengeance. More than hating organized crime, crooked judges, cops, politicians, the indifferent public, or anything like that. It's become something more than any of us or even the sum of all our efforts. It's like seeing someone you love being eaten alive with cancer and knowing you can save them by cutting out that cancer...and then doing it, no matter how much it hurts to carve it away."

Mark sighed deeply again. "But, come on inside. We have a dry run to go through and then a midnight rehearsal of our penetration. Time to hit 'em again."

8

DEATH WATCH

HOT DAMN, YOU COULDN'T PICK A WORSE FRIGGIN' time for a set like this; no moon and blacker than the hem of a nun's habit. Nothin' to see, nothin' to know for sure. Chu-Chu Lavagni had placed his boys all around the four-block square area in the City of Commerce. Now they had nothing to do until or unless this hotshot outfit that had been knocking over the LA boys like tenpins showed. Hell of a deal it was too. None of his guys could get within two blocks of the place where Ollivetti had said he and his two boys would be parked.

Chu-Chu was getting restless. He'd reported to Stan the Man by radio telephone that everyone was in place. That was it. Not once, since they had all come up from San Diego, had Ollivetti come over to the hard site to check with them. Everything had been done by telephone. Hell of a way to do a job. But, what the shit, the extra head pay to him and every member of his crew made it worth the deal. He settled back in his seat and fired up a short, black Italian cigar.

Chu-Chu had it figured for a waste of time. This super-rodman Hardin and his faithful Indian companion Tonto...Bullshit! An old Indian with a bow and arrows! Bullshit! Well, let them show up and he'd give them both a Little Big Horn. Yeah, a big horn right up their tails!

Tutti and Frutti Gambini were sitting in the front seat of Stan Ollivetti's black Cad, each watching a different approach to the fenced-in parking lot in which they were parked. Stan leaned back in the plush cushions of the rear seat and smiled with satisfaction. Lavagni had reported his men in position around the place, the grease was in with the local night-shift cops, and all was ready. He checked his watch and saw that he was still fifteen minutes early. So what? They had this Mr. Smart-ass Hardin right where they wanted him. No danger of a mistake this time.

Chu-Chu Lavagni heard the soft throb of the helicopter blades as the craft settled into the dark lot, its running lights doused to insure secrecy. Looked like he was right, Lavagni noted, the whirlybird was here and no sign of another car in the area. This Hardin character wasn't going to show. The chopper settled to the ground, a darker form against darkness, disappearing behind the bulk of the warehouse.

Then there was a sudden brightness, like maybe one of them H bombs going off. What the hell, thought they wanted this to be all so secret. The chopper took off. So soon? It came back again, settling down behind the warehouse into that awful glare. The light was going out and the chopper was leaving again. Chu-Chu was curious, but not so curious that he would investigate without definite word from the boss man. His lack of curiosity saved his life.

As the Mafia helicopter settled to the ground, swaying slightly on its springy undercarriage, Mark Hardin rose up from behind the parapet of the warehouse roof where he had been deposited by Larry Novak shortly after dark. He pointed the big 40mm tube downward and fired the flare gun. Quickly he kicked open the breech, ejecting the spent casing and inserting another magnesium flare, snapping the gun closed and firing it. He had already flipped into place the special smoke-filter goggles, and now the scene below him became frozen, strobelike, as the flares went off.

Caught in the space between car and helicopter, arms flung upward to protect night-dilated eyes from the hellish brightness of the flares, were Stan the Man, his two bodyguards and a stocky Chinese.

The frozen instant passed and, dropping the bundle containing the heroin shipment, the Chinese snatched the briefcase from Stan's fingers and dashed for the chopper.

Mark quickly filled his hand with the .22 High Standard and it phutted a stinging pellet toward the fleeing Chinaman. The tiny 40-grain slug caught him near the elbow of his left arm, causing him to drop the briefcase full of money. He sprinted the last few feet and dived through the open hatch as a second slug gouged a trough along his back, from left buttock to right shoulder, spattering harmlessly off the control column. As the bird lifted, Mark turned back to the scene below.

The three Mafiosi had recovered enough to pull their heat, but could only look about in blinded confusion. The sweet little Trophy Model coughed again—then twice more in rapid succession—and Tutti Gambini fell face-first to the blacktop surface of the lot. Stan Ollivetti started for his Cadillac, intent on reaching the radio and the comparative safety of its interior. Mark cut his feet out from under him with a shot to the right knee. Ollivetti was stunned by the fall.

Mark brought his attention back to Frutti Gambini, where he knelt, bending over his dead brother. He ended the bodyguard's problems and his life with two hollow point .22s through the top of his head. The vengeance-seeking gunner returned his fistful of softly chuffing death to its holster and grasping a nylon rope rigged earlier rappelled down the face of the warehouse. Drawing the silenced blaster again, replacing the magazine with a full one, he cautiously approached the fallen form of Stan the Man Ollivetti.

Stan the Man was nearly halfway across the space between his Cad and the chopper and the Chinaman was directly in front of him when, with soft pops the magnesium flares detonated a few feet above the ground. "What the fuck!" he gasped, throwing his arm over his face to protect his eyes from the searing pain caused by sudden brightness. He felt a tugging at his other arm and sensed rather than saw the Chinaman drop his bundle and grab the money. He heard footsteps slap-slapping across the blacktop and a grunt of pain from the Chinese, then the chopper roared and lifted from the ground.

He jerked out his own rod, shading his eyes, straining to see beyond the glare. Then Stan heard the unmistakable meaty smack of slugs hitting flesh and Tutti Gambini fell.

"Christ! Oh, Christ!" Federico Gambini cried out as his brother fell dead. He brushed past his boss and went to his knees beside his twin.

"Forget him," Stan the Man cried. "Get the bastard! Get that Hardin bastard!"

Ollivetti looked around. Where was his bodyguard? Like a nine-year-old at his first communion, he was beside his brother praying. "Hail Mary, full of grace..." It was all too unreal. The mumbled prayer, the ungodly bright light, the silenced gun spitting death from nowhere, all of it contrived to make a waking nightmare. And, nightmare-like, Stan Ollivetti moved as in a dream, slowly at first, turning toward his car and starting to run for it. But like a man under water, he was not moving fast enough at all.

"...God, pray for us sinners now and at the hour of..."

Phut! Phut! From somewhere a stinging hornet bit into the back of Stan the Man's right knee and he sprawled face-first onto the hard macadam lot. Blackness whirled in his head, fogging the bright light.

Fighting unconsciousness, he shook his head. Frantically, he tried to clear his mind and his vision. Then, before him, like another part of a bad dream, was a man all in black, turtleneck sweater, black Levi's, black boots, the black, grotesque muzzle of a silencer unwaveringly directed toward his head. Hopelessly, Stan the Man lifted a hand, as if to ward off the bullet. A red-orange flower bloomed and hot lead kissed his cheek. Stan Ollivetti fell back, feebly trying to bring his own gun to bear. He heard what he thought was their chopper returning and rallied his resources. Reflexively, his finger twitched and he got off a shot. It went wide of his mark and the silencer coughed again. White-hot, stabbing pain slammed into his chest, like a nail driven into flesh. His head hit the pavement and blackness came over him as the big man in black picked up the heroin from where it had fallen.

But Stan the Man was past caring, past knowing what had happened to his well-laid plans, past even realizing that he had just had a close look at the man responsible for the destruction of those plans. He was one with the darkness...

Mark Hardin heard the approaching throb of Larry Novak's chopper and he crouched to retrieve the heroin shipment. Running bent over, he snatched up the case of cash and dodged into the open cockpit. He gave the pilot a quick "thumbs up" signal, sending the helicopter into the air again. Stowing the gear behind him, Mark removed his smoke goggles and grinned at the ex-Mafia henchman.

"That'll sure as hell throw them for a loop. Now's the time to gain yardage. I think I want a close look at Don Pietro. A real close look."

9
SEVEN MILLION STRAWS

THIS WAS MORE LIKE IT! A PERSONAL SUMMONS from Don Pietro Scarelli to come to the Don's house in the swell district. Chu-Chu Lavagni was more than pleased with himself. That standoffish bastard Ollivetti wouldn't even come over to visit the two crews Lavagni had brought up from Diego, but now someone with class was giving the orders.

It was still early morning when Chu-Chu left the hard site to drive across the sprawling LA basin to Beverly Hills. Everything was going just perfect. He was to make a report on the night before and the botch that Stan the Man had made of the transfer. Nothing could dampen the enthusiasm the Mafia gunman felt that morning. Not even that drunk in the little Jap car that kept tailgating him.

Weaving and honking, the small sports model leaned on it in earnest as Lavagni turned off onto the narrow, road identified as Westwood Drive. They rounded several turns so close together, it was as if the little car were being towed. Then, with an angry snarl of exhaust, the RX-3 poured on the coal and whipped around Lavagni's Chrysler 300, barely missing contact between the small car's rear fender and the big chrome bumper on the Mafiosi's car. Bending backward, eyes off the road, the drunken driver of the small foreign job made an obscene gesture at Lavagni.

"Rich bastards," the San Diego gunman growled. "They'll get theirs."

He was right. He had driven around only two more curves in the winding, uphill road, when he hit the brakes hard to avoid a collision with the little bright yellow Mazda. It was now sideways across both lanes of the road, shoved up against the bank. The door was open on the driver's side and the drunk now lay sprawled outside, his head resting on the blacktop. Chu-Chu got out and walked ponderously over to the other car.

"Gawddamn, have to move him to get this heap outta my way," he griped aloud as he came up to the apparently unconscious driver. Bending down, he grabbed the man by one shoulder and lifted to heave him inside the little car. When he did, he found himself looking into the unblinking black eye of a silencer.

Mark's High Standard pfutted twice, the first slug taking Lavagni in his open mouth. His next shot entered the right eye, expending its energy among the rapidly dying brain cells as Chu-Chu Lavagni caught up with the fate he had escaped the night before.

Mark was up and moving before the big man's body hit the ground. He dragged the corpse to the trunk of the Chrysler and flopped Lavagni inside, closing the lid securely. Behind him, David Red Eagle emerged from the passenger's side of the RX-3 and started the car, backing it and heading off down the road. He gave Mark a wave of encouragement before rounding the bend.

Mark drove Chu-Chu's Chrysler on toward Don Pietro's palatial home until he found a narrow side lane. He turned off the main road and followed this street until he was satisfied he could not be seen from Westwood Drive. He got out and opened the trunk removing all identification and money from Lavagni's slowly cooling corpse.

"Well, well," he exclaimed aloud. "A private ticket." It identified Gregory Lavagni as a member of Angel's Security Service in San Diego. There was also a California driver's license made out to the same name. He studied the photos on both licenses carefully, then removed from his inside coat pocket a compact makeup kit. Working quickly, he set about changing his appearance.

He relied on the popular belief that official photographs never really looked like the person portrayed. His clothes had been well chosen, a dark blue shirt, white tie, dark slacks, white buck loafers and electric blue socks. He wore almost an exact duplicate of what the corpse wore. With a little difficulty, he removed the dead man's sports jacket, a lighter blue than either trousers or shirt. It was a nearly perfect fit. He returned his silenced .22 to the shoulder rig and added his Colt Commander to the right-hand waistband of his trousers.

Checking the mirror, he made final adjustments to his new face and got behind the wheel. He hummed a few bars of Sorrento as he turned around and headed back to Westwood Drive. After all, Chu-Chu Lavagni had an appointment with Don Pietro and it wouldn't do to arrive late.

Pulling slowly up the wide, curving drive to the front door of Pete Scarelli's rambling home, Mark appreciated for the first time what all that dirty money could do for a person. This was wealth, position and power. No amateur squeeze play was going to jar the Don lose from all the security represented by this place. The door to the house opened as Mark stopped and cut the motor.

"Who you?" inquired a scarred and muscular guy blocking the front door.

"Chu-Chu Lavagni," Mark told him. "Don Pietro wants to see me."

"In a pig's ass. You got identification?"

"Sure, meathead. How's this?" Mark withdrew Lavagni's wallet with his left hand and flipped it to the bodyguard. The muscle-bound one examined the photographs on both driver's license and the private investigator's ID. He didn't toss back the wallet.

"You got somethin' else?" he grunted. "Money, maybe?"

"You shakin' a little down on the side, punk?"

"I'll punk your ass for you. Come on, give."

"Look, I'm Gregory Lavagni from San Diego, we was over at the hard site, me and the two crews I command. Don Pietro himself called, said he wanted to see me...oh, oh yeah," Mark ground to a halt as it came to him at last. He reached into his trouser pocket and removed his money clip, bulging with large denomination bills. Its center was a twenty-dollar gold piece. "Ya mean this kind of money?"

At once, the bodyguard's manner changed, changed so drastically he seemed to become a proper butler. "Yes, sir, Mister Lavagni. Come right this way, sir." He returned Mark's wallet and the twenty-dollar piece Mark had thrown him. Tiger Palwalski was worried. In all of his years—first as a boxer owned by Don Pietro and later as a member of his household staff—Tiger had never braced one of the biggies before. Now he had really done it. He was expecting a crew chief. Expected at the most to see a five-dollar gold coin, more likely a silver dollar. He went over his conversation, hoping that he had not violated proper "respect" for this important visitor.

Similar thoughts went through Mark's head as he was led down a long hall, open on both sides to large, well-lit, tastefully decorated rooms. He was sure now that he would be accepted without question by the entire palace guard and any other staff he might run into. His big test would be confronting the Don himself. His wiretap on Ollivetti's hard site had paid off with this opportunity and he was determined to make the most of it, come what may. To be able to meet the coming test, he spared a grateful thought for Don Alberto Rizzo, from whom he had acquired his gold piece legitimately, so many years ago. The twenty-dollar gold piece was a special sign of high, trust, a badge of identification for those who—though not always Sicilian—were high in Family rank and esteem.

At thc door to Don Pietro's study, the butler/ bodyguard patted down his visitor.

"Uh-uh, that's not polite," Mark said in a bantering tone.

"Just routine, sir. You always carry two guns?"

"Sometimes. You want them before I go in?"

"No, sir. Not necessary. Just as long as everyone knows when anyone else is packing." He knocked softly. "You may enter, sir. You are expected."

"Thanks much."

Inside the study, Don Pietro Scarelli waited behind his massive desk. As the stranger entered, he took a long, slow drag from his ice water, using the time to study this crew boss from San Diego. He liked what he saw. Hard, purposeful lines in the face, dark skin and the features of a born fighter. Why couldn't the right Families in LA produce one such as this? Hell, half the kids who should be coming into Our Thing these days were pansy. “Lavagni?” he asked the newcomer.

“Yes, sir. It’s a pleasure to make your acquaintance, Don Pietro. Don Angelo has great respect for you, as do all of us in San Diego.”

“And I have the deepest respect for Don Angelo. How is he?”

“Excellent, sir. Best of health. He and his family, are all doing well.”

The old Don took another sip of water. “Good. Now that we’ve had at least a minimum of attention to form, let’s get to business. Sit down.”

Mark Hardin took a chair opposite the Don. He paid close attention to the knife sharp creases in his trousers. So far his hasty disguise had held. Here he was, inside with The Man. His silence was taken as respect.

“So. What happened down there? I send my best man, set up a bunch of you to cover the area, and what happens?” Don Pietro gestured widely, hands out, palms up.

“Well, Don Pietro, Mister Ollivetti made us all stay at least two blocks away. He and his two boys went in to where it was they were to meet. So, until we hear a shot, how we to know, I mean, he never told us how it was to go.”

“Yeah. Sure,” the older man replied. It was much the same story he had pieced together in the early morning hours following the foul-up at the warehouse. “With him still in The Home,” he went on, “no way to hear why he did dumb things before this evening.” It was the first Mark knew that his aim had been off; that Stan Ollivetti had survived. His mind spun, trying to analyze the importance of this new bit of information. He realized something more was expected. "My boys, Don Pietro. We are still here. How do you want to use us?"

Pietro Scarelli thought a few moments. "We gotta find this guy and put an end to this. With him on the loose, no telling what he could do next. I need you here. Bring over some of the boys, beef up the operation. Keep the rest handy." He frowned, sipped again from the water before continuing. "I suppose you heard we lost a large shipment of junk last night. The friggin' money too. We want it all back. So, I want this guy alive and talkin'. I want back what's mine."

"Right, Don Pietro. We'll do what we can. Count on us to help in any way you want."

"Good boy. I think we're gonna get along real well. You had anything to eat?"

"No, sir. I come right over when you called."

"Go out to the kitchen. Tell the cook you want breakfast. My house manager's there. You two get to know each other real good. I want you to get along like two guys in one skin, so we can make sure of this bastard."

"Yes, sir," Mark stood, the interview was over. With a final handshake, he left the study.

Mark was finishing his third cup of coffee. Filled with ham, eggs and freshly baked bread, he felt fine. Around him were the men of the Don's household. Shep Lorca, the house manager, had been anxious to cooperate, giving an estimate of how many men would be needed to seal up the entire estate. Openly cooperative, he also informed Mark of how many men were currently at the Westwood Drive address. He tookanother sip of coffee as two hard men drifted into the kitchen, grabbing hunks of fresh bread and cups of coffee.

"I tell ya, Angie," one confided to the other, "findin' this guy before he knocks over anything else is like lookin' for a needle in a haystack."

"You're right there...only this stack's got seven million straws."

"How you mean?"

"LA has seven million people, dummy, right? And do we know what this putano looks like? No! See what I mean?"

"Like that huh? You know how to make it rough for a guy," his companion agreed. "Shit, man, we haven't even gone out lookin' for him since that thing in the desert."

"You in a hurry to go where The Musician went? See what he got for his efforts. Now, Stan the Man is all shot up. They say he got his cheek opened up from his mouth almost to his ear. Just like with a knife: Hole through his ear too. And he has to use a cane—if they even let him out today. Too early, if you ask me."

"Sure wish we knew who this guy was," the other said. He turned to Mark. "You got any ideas?"

Mark shrugged. "Hard to say. Hell, it could even be me."

"Not in here it couldn't. Who are you anyway?"

"You better remember his face," Shep Lorca interjected. "That's Chu-Chu Lavagni from Diego...Mister Lavagni to you two."

They mumbled their gladtameetchas and conversation turned to the crews up from San Diego. As they went along, Mark inventing to cover his ignorance of Family operations in California's First City, there was a flurry of movement at the hallway door. Into the room walked Stan, the Man Ollivetti.

His right cheek and ear were bandaged and he held his shoulders gingerly, Mark's bullet had hit a rib and been deflected, hitting nothing vital. He walked with a cane and his right knee was grotesquely large from, yet another surgical dressing. He had no business being out of bed, had in fact left the private hospital where Family wounded were cared for in secret by a "tame" doctor against orders and was now standing there, glaring at the men around the big table.

His eyes settled on Mark. He was curious at first-then confused—at least a growing recognition came to his eyes. His face flushed red with anger and he opened his maimed mouth to try to tell the others. Let them know that somehow, some way, that arrogant son of a bitch that had hit them the previous night was right here among them, sopping up coffee and BS'ing the troops. "Kriz!" the words came out in a muffled growl. Pointing his finger at Mark, he struggled to make himself clear. "Ass du un! Ass sonbish du un!" His empty hand darted toward the front of his jacket.

Caught unawares, the street soldiers around the table only gaped—first at the bandaged apparition in the door and then at the target of his garbled shouts. They were slow in reacting, slow to understand what it was Stan Ollivetti was saying. Then, they too clawed for their blasters.

Mark wasn't that slow. He had realized he had to play it pretty close from the time Don Pietro had informed him Ollivetti wasn't dead. He had reasoned that if he was found here when the Capo returned it would be pretty sticky. Well, it was more than sticky now. He had his big .45 out and the hammer falling long before the two palace guards recovered. His first shot finished the job he had begun the night before, catching Stan Ollivetti squarely in the chest, slamming him back through the swinging door into a wall, where he hung for a moment, before slowly sliding downward to the floor and into oblivion.

The barking roar of the big gun had frozen the others in the room halfway between standing and sitting. Mark judged correctly which target presented the next most dangerous threat; he sent a whistling .45 slug into Shep Lorca's startled face, spraying brain tissue out the back of his head. Blood, bone and bits of tissue splattered on the stocky, rotund Italian cook and she went into hysterics. Her scream rose in a piercing wail as Mark unlimbered another shot, this time at the brighter of the two soldiers at the table with him. The thinker died as his gun cleared leather, flipping backward over his chair with a third eye in the center of his forehead.

Mark pivoted and snapped off two shots into the city-soft body of the other gunsel as he began a retreat through the rear door. He could hear shouts in the front of the house, pounding footsteps on the rear stairs and more coming down the hall toward the kitchen. All the holes were rapidly being plugged. Barely one jump ahead of the reinforcements coming down the rear stairs, Mark jerked open the back door.

He spun to make his exit and came face to face with a giant of a man holding a double twelve-gauge sawed off. Mark let his left knee go out from under him, dropping low and left—falling away from the right-handed man and his ten-inch shotgun—as he emptied his last three shots into the giant's middle. The two-hundred-grain Hensley and Gibbs soft-lead slugs made heavy smacking sounds as they punched into flesh, their force—so near the muzzle-throwing Mark's target left and backward through the porch railing into a flower bed. He was dead. Mark vaulted the opposite side railing and hugged the building for cover. Switching to his silenced pistol, he checked his movement a second to see what would develop.

It wasn't long in coming. Two guys skidded around the corner of the house and into hell as the High Standard coughed rapidly four times and red spots—like tiny pimples—appeared on their faces. Mark used the time he felt he had gained to make a rush to the back door of a cabana near the backyard swimming pool. He wrenched the handle and it gave, admitting him to its dubious shelter. Three slugs slammed into the building behind him and he doubled back long enough to lock the door from the inside.

As Mark stepped through the door on the pool side of the cabana, another hard man charged toward him from the shrubbery on the opposite side. Hollow point death sped to meet him and he continued his charge—triggering two shots into the air from his .380 Beretta. He plunged into the pool...too dead to care about getting wet.

The chances were running out for Mark. He had to go one way or the other and time said the odds were he'd get his either way. He chose the far end, more removed from the house, and sprinted toward it. His mind flashed on the giddy, senseless thought that they were in the last seconds of the game and there were no officials to call time out. Bullets whined off cement and ricocheted from the diving tower as he reached his goal. Elbows high to shield his face, he plunged into the thick green hedge. Searing pain flared suddenly along the left side of his chest and he bit off an involuntary cry of anguish.

"Hey! I hit him," a voice called from behind him.

More shots poured in, all of them far too close. Then Mark felt himself stumbling, pitching forward to fall in the damp leaves and grass on the other side of the hedge. He hit with a passable snap roll and came up; examining his foot to find the heel of one shoe had been shot off. He pulled off both shoes and started out again, but his efforts had been too great. His head swam, blackness rushed in and he tumbled to the ground again. Behind him he heard more voices as men gathered to push through the hedge after him. Stickiness from the blood running down his side jerked him back and he began to run and kept on running....

10
OFFICIAL SPOTLIGHT

Little cartoon bugs drummed their heels and gasped their last in living color, after they were attacked by the kindly, smiling can of bug spray. The scene slowly faded, to be replaced by a still photograph of a man seated at a long conference table, surrounded by press representatives. The camera dollied back to show the familiar grizzled figure of CBS News' top man in New York.

"In an unprecedented move tonight, Senator Marvyn Corvus called a special session of the Subcommittee on Crime and Violence," the commentator's voice rumbled in bass register. "Following the session, newsmen were admitted to the committee room, where the Senator made the following statement: As a result of the events of this afternoon and early evening, our committee has decided to take the matter of gangland war in Los Angeles under direct investigation. The committee will be leaving tomorrow morning for California where we shall conduct a long, searching investigation into the events of the past month. We consider it of gravest concern that violence has been allowed to continue unchecked. Senator Corvus went on to say that he did not wish to give the impression he was casting aspersions on the competence or honesty of local authorities in Los Angeles. It was merely that he felt it was time for Federal intervention.

"The Senator's decision was apparently spurred by the attack early today on the home of Southern California Loan Company chain executive, Peter Scarelli, by an unknown number of persons. We will have on-the-spot coverage of this situation on the eleven o'clock..."

In Los Angeles, Channel Eleven, not being a network affiliate, was well into the local news. "Police continue their investigation of a reported shooting incident near the home of prominent financial figure, Peter Scarelli," the announcer informed his audience. "Despite denials made by loan company magnate, Scarelli, of any gunplay in or around his home, police are now making inquiries regarding a report of a tall, lean man, with a big gun, seen fleeing the area near the time of the reported shooting. Two persons, at least, who spoke with reporters, indicated they believed the fleeing man to be wounded.

"This is just another in a seemingly continuous series of gangland incidents over the past month here in our Southland." The reporter had removed his glasses and, with myopic seriousness, he peered directly into the camera as he continued with editorial fervor. "Our question tonight is not directed at what may have brought this about. Nor is it, 'Who is responsible?' What we—and I believe all the law-abiding residents of Southern California—want to know is: When will something be done to stop it? Let's hope the police keep that question uppermost in their minds. Meanwhile, we'll keep you posted on any late-breaking information here on Channel Eleven."

"It would appear that perhaps you have gone a bit too far, too fast, my boy," Willard Haskins commented dryly.

"It was not the plan. He was looking for information only," David Red Eagle said in Mark's defense. He had just finished tying bandages around the younger man's chest, re-dressing the flesh wound Mark had received during his escape from Don Pietro's home. It had bled a lot, but wasn't serious.

"Yes," Mark concurred. "With the Feds in this, it might be better to lay off a while. This is something we didn't consider."

"You've hurt them all, my boy. Crippled the criminal element in Los Angeles and rubbed it in the noses of the police...and left a considerable number of bodies scattered across the landscape. If you want the advice of an old, addled professor, I would suggest that you take the time to go back to your conditioning activities for a while. You have stirred up enough of a mess, let us hope it will allow the police to catch the rest of these fish in their net."

"Maybe you are right. You know, I promised to get a hundred of them for Donna. Well, I've lost count. In fact, I don't even bother to count any more. Just might be time to take it easy."

"Kelly, I want you to meet Dan Griggs. Dan's with Senator Corvus's committee on violence. He will be chief counsel and will head the team of investigators." Paul Harris made the introductions.

"Pleased to meet you, Dan," Kelly replied sincerely. "I've admired the Senator for a long time. I must say your approach is a lot better than that gang from the State Department."

Dan Griggs, short and slim to the point of being skinny, flashed even, white teeth in laughing agreement. "You mean the very proper Mister Taylor? When the Senator announced he was making a special investigation of this situation, prissy Miss Taylor came over to demand we not do it. He had ominous things to say about serious international repercussions. Nuts! If some cannibal in the Congo farts, those State Department johnnies analyze it to see if it will have serious international repercussions."

Kelly felt warm acceptance of this shrewd little lawyer. "That's about the way I figure it too. Nice to have you around. My office is out near Topanga Canyon —where the first hit was made—but the Lieutenant here has duplicates of all my reports and everything so far. Want to work here?"

"I'd work better after a steak and a martini. Join me?"

"You're on," Kelly replied.

"The Senator won't be here until tomorrow and the first day of hearings isn't scheduled before next week, so we have a lot of time to get used to each other. I'll try not to step on your toes, if you'll try not to accuse me of being a politician first and an investigator second. Deal?"

"Deal."

Just down from the civic center area of Los Angeles is Olvera Street. It is right off the old Town Plaza, and it boasts shops, restaurants and architecture dating back to the time of the Spanish. Among them is Restaurante Chapultapec. It was there that Kelly led the man from Washington. The interior was as rustic as the outside. Adobe-block walls were hung with wrought-iron wall sconces; there was an open beam ceiling, and plank tables held traditional clay bowls of pickled jalapeño peppers, carrots and onions, and savory red salsa bran made of chopped tomatoes, garlic, hot peppers and other spices. A native of the area and a fan of Mexican food, Kelly took a corn-chip frito from another bowl and scooped up the fiery sauce.

"Don't try it, unless you can take it hot," he advised Dan Griggs. "Me, I eat it by the spoonful."

"Buenos noches, señores," an attractive young waitress appeared at their table.

"Muy buenas noches, Consuelo," Kelly replied. The girl covered her mouth with one hand as a giggle escaped her. Kelly was a regular in the place, but his unintentional and unnoticed Irish lilt made Spanish a foreign language to the Mexican staff. "Quiero carnitas y tien esto Señor carne asada, medio, por favor."

Writing quickly, between giggles, Consuelo took their order. "And," Dan interjected, "a pitcher of cold, very dry martinis, a bowl of olives and two cold glasses."

"You weren't kidding about that martini, were you?" Kelly grinned.

"No other way to think about all this. Is it true your department suspects a single two-man team of all these hits?"

"Right. At least the Lieutenant and I do. If we're correct, the guy in charge has a hellish proficiency with military weapons. Civilian arms too. In fact, he seems to prefer civilian weapons. Then, to add insult to injury, we have no difficulty identifying the barrels he's fired the slugs from. On one occasion he casually removed the barrel of his .45 and tossed it on the chest of his victim. So we can't tie down one weapon to any of the hits. Whatever the case, he sure is cutting a broad swath through the Mafia in this area."

"Please! Don't use that word. In official Washingtonese it is organized criminal activity. Must never offend any ethnic group these days, you know." Dan changed his tone, from light banter to seriousness. "This guy of yours has sure captured the headlines. All sorts of pressure is being brought down on us in D.C. And never one to leave an opportunity unseized, the Senator has naturally climbed aboard. If there was ever a time for a Federal police force it's now."

Kelly scowled. "You're talking to the wrong man to get any agreement on that."

"A Federal task force on organized crime, then," the little lawyer amended. "That, I might go along with."

Their drinks arrived and talk turned to homes, families and the nature of their work. Sizzling platters of food were brought. Dan Griggs gingerly tried the hot salsa and found he liked it, even while it brought beads of perspiration to his forehead and tears to his eyes. By the time everything was reduced to scraps, both men were feeling mellow.

"Seriously, the hell of it all is that we just don't have a line on this guy," Kelly told the Washington man, as they walked through the bar area on their way out.

"Well, he can't be in it alone. The guy has to have a base of operations, finances, lines of communication. He has to have information sources. What about hitting those? But you are right. He could have been right next to us at dinner and we'd never have known," Dan concluded.

Special Investigator Dan Griggs never realized how accurate his suggestion was. A distinguished-looking, gray-haired gentleman at the bar nodded and smiled to them as they passed. He took another sip of his Tullamore Dew Irish whiskey and swiveled on the stool to watch their passage out of the restaurant. Professor Willard Haskins was collecting intelligence data on the opposition and was now anxious to return with his report. It would prove very interesting indeed....

11

THE DEVIL TO PAY

"So, we at least have a neutral in this Sheriff's Department guy. Nice to know," Mark Hardin commented as he applied rubber cement to the last slip of paper and attached it to a larger sheet. "Your report on the guy from D.C. is interesting, though. Like it or not, with the Feds taking this much interest, we have to accelerate our moves, rather than take cover and let them figure it all out for themselves. They have the resources and the manpower to dig me out fast.

"How do you like this?" he asked as he extended the product of his past hour's labor.

Willard Haskins took the page and examined it closely. Made up from words clipped out of newspapers and magazines, the message read:

WILL SELL BACK YOUR H FOR $250,000
WILL DEAL WITH TOP MAN ONLY

THE DON OR FORGET IT! YOU ARE WATCHED YOU RECEIVE DIRECTIONS SOON

"My God! You seem to have a natural flare for ransom notes, my boy," the older man exclaimed. "Pity all of that talent is going to waste to return that deadly powder."

"Who said anything about returning the heroin? It's just another way of tapping the Mafia till for a quarter million dollars."

"Provided they go for it."

"They will, they will. One way or another."

Two days later, Don Pietro Scarelli slammed his big fist onto his desk, pinning Mark's ransom, note beneath it. "What the hell! This punk of all punks! He'll return my smack for a quarter million! What kinda shit are you guys up to, he can get away with this?"

There was the usual round of disclaimers from those in the study. Don Pietro's eyes smoldered with seething anger. He paced back and forth a few times, sipped his inevitable ice water and sat heavily in his chair.

"Hell, I can't blame you guys. Right here in this office he was. I even liked the guy, he looks so good for who he turns out to be. I'll never forget that face, though. Never. So what do we do now?"

"Maybe we should set up a little reception committee for this wise-ass?" Tug Boat Donnelson suggested. As crew chief of the Vegas contingent, he had inherited leadership over the out-of-town talent.

"Sure, sure," agreed the Don. "But first this guy has to..." He was interrupted by a ringing phone.

"Scarelli?" came the voice over the phone.

"You got him," replied the Don, nodding his head to signal the other that it was the expected call.

"You want your stuff back, here's how it will be."

"Wait a minute. How do I know you are the real goods?"

"You drink ice water, keep it on your desk. You have a genuine Picasso behind the desk on the side wall of your study and your short, fat Italian cook makes fantastic fresh bread each day."

"Son of a bitch! For that I never forgive you. You shootin' up this place, she went hysterical on us. Quit me cold. I'll never find another one like her." There was a dry chuckle from the other end. "Satisfied? Here's how it will be. You know where Rossmore runs by the Wilshire Country Club? Well, tonight at eleven-thirty sharp, you be there. Come alone and bring the money. I'll pass off the stuff. Got that?"

"How do I know you won't hit me?"

Again the dry chuckle. "If I had intended to snuff you, you'd have gone first the other day. You know damn well I had a silencer on one of my guns. Think about it."

There were several seconds of silence. Don Pietro clenched his teeth so tightly that his lips were white rimmed. At last he nodded to himself. "Right. Eleven-thirty. I'll be there." The line went dead.

Donnelson rubbed his hands in anticipation as the Don explained the nature of Mark's phone call. "We got him now, the sonofabitch!" he cried. "I know that area from before when I operated here. I can put boys all over that joint. No sweat, sir. We can stake out some guys in those shrubs along Rossmore and..."

Vine Street ends at Beverly Boulevard and becomes Rossmore. From there, it winds in a gentle curve around the eastern border of the Wilshire Country Club. Along the street are many tall, stately apartment houses, many of brick and brownstone. To shelter the famous and not so famous from the prying eyes of the neighborhood, the Country Club has a tall hedge that runs the length of a high chain-link fence dividing their property from the remainder of the city. This is considered one of the "better" neighborhoods, sparsely lighted and casually patrolled by units from Wilcox Division of the L.A.P.D. It was ideal for a, meet, or for an ambush. Mark Hardin took precautions accordingly.

Rattling along in David Red Eagle's battered old pickup, the rear filled with gardening tools, Mark was far from the expected target as he cased the lay of the set. His glittering black eyes took in furtive movements among the bushes of the tall hedge, a carelessly lit cigarette in one spot, cars left near intersections, seemingly empty but with all the windows rolled down. All of the usual indications of an ambush set up by comparative amateurs. Not so amateurish at the game of killing, yet still not accustomed to the rigid discipline of a military ambush.

Mark cruised the area three times, determining the positions of nearly all of the Mafia types awaiting his arrival. At one point, he even stopped beside a car that betrayed a glowing cigar tip and asked directions. He grinned in self-satisfaction at his parting shot. "You cops sure got it easy. All you have to do is sit around; Me, I have to sweat for a living. Jeez." The hoods had made startled, half-laughing replies to being identified as police.

The time had arrived. Mark parked his vehicle, slipped into a pair of green coveralls and collected his weapons. He selected the silenced High Standard, a single phosphorous grenade and plenty of ammunition. Silently, on crepe soles, he slipped between the darkened apartment buildings and returned to Rossmore. He took his stand behind n large pine tree at the front of a brick apartment house.

Cautiously he examined the street, reorienting himself on the positions of the enemy. Satisfied that none of them had moved, he quickly mapped out a course of action. Directly across from him was the careless smoker. He figured to start with him. As he raised the silencer-tipped pistol, a voice from near him startled the noiseless penetrator. "Don't get trigger-happy, buddy. Donnelson said we take this guy alive—not in one piece, but alive. That settles that."

Mark located the owner of the voice and turned the deadly muzzle toward him. He settled the officious button man with two well-placed shots in the head. Just then, a match flared across the street. Mark zeroed in on its light and snapped off two more. shots. Discipline ceased to be a problem for the careless smoker. He went down with a strangled cry.

"Hey! What's that?" called another voice.

"Down here! He's hitting us!" yet another hood cried.

Lights flared from a car down the block. Mark took aim at the car just across the street from him and carefully pumped three low ricocheting shots into the gas tank. "Somebody's shootin' at the car," came a shout from inside.

"Down there, he's heading our way," Mark shouted as the other car roared to life. The ambushers began to pour a steady stream of fire into the approaching car. The hard men inside, naturally, returned fire. Mark figured enough time had elapsed so he gently lobbed the WP grenade under the car across the street. It burst with a blinding glare and a satisfying whumpf as the spilled gas ignited.

Inside the doomed car, men screamed in terror and tumbled out the doors, to be met with more shots from their unseen attacker. Part way up the street a good firefight had developed between other of the button men so Mark concentrated on the burning car. As another occupant leaped for safety, he sprawled face-first in the street, his head and chest punctured by three sizzling .22 hollow points. Other guys broke concealment to rush to the aid of those trapped by the flames. As they become moving silhouettes against the ruddy glow, one by one they fell to Mark's well-aimed shots.

Firing now broke out from the other end of the ambush and Mark decided it was time to pull the pin. He faded back into the darkness at the side of the brick apartment, covering his rear as he went. Once in the alley, he turned and trotted quietly between two buildings facing on the other street and found Red Eagle's pickup. He removed the coveralls, concealed his weapons and started up the old truck.

A block away, with sounds of battle growing behind him, he stopped to pull an alarm box, sending the fire department to the scene of action. He also removed the barrel of the High Standard and tossed it down a storm drain, reminding himself that he had not policed up his brass and would have to change firing pin, and extractor when he returned to The Stronghold.

Dropping the old buggy into gear, he drove serenely away to a chorus of sirens. Already his mind was occupied with how to make Don Pietro pay even more for this ambush. And pay he would.

12
THE GANG'S ALL HERE

"I AM SURE SOME OF YOU MAY FIND THIS A MATTER of inconvenience." The words came, in their slightly bored upper-class English intonation, over a speaker sitting on Don Pietro's desk. "It is, however, the most reliable manner of maintaining our anonymity. I hope the gentlemen from France and our Chinese friend find their quarters comfortable." Other voices joined His Lordship's in agreement. "It is time to get to business."

Don Pietro fiddled with a gold pencil as His Lordship took a long pause. "Mister Scarelli, I am really amazed that you and your men find it so difficult to isolate and eliminate a single man. Is it still your contention that only one man is involved?"

The Mafia leader bit back a sharp retort before he could reply. "Yes. You bet it's one guy. But what a hell of a guy he is. I've seen him. I'd like to have with us."

"I am sure you realize that is far from possible," Chau Li interrupted. "The People's Republic has lost one courier, which has excited the attention of the Federals and we have one man wounded. I am of a mind to end this venture."

"Now just a minute," Don Pietro started.

"Unless and until your men can contain this menace," His Lordship fired back, "I am afraid there is no ground upon which we can conduct further business. For my own part, I am helping as much as I can. In the field, openly, you are the only one who can move, Peter. The purpose of this meeting is to lay plans that will insure the capture of this Hardin person."

"Messieurs, although your operation has made inroads in our profit base, it has had its compensations. Much of the pressure is off our network to New York. If the Chinese gentleman desires to remove his country's interest—in order to, ah, save face? I can assure you that the possibility exists that we might be able to supply your network with ample merchandise directly from our processing facilities in Marseilles."

"Face is not the issue here," the Chinese snapped. "If this business venture was ever connected with the People's Republic of China, it would have serious repercussions, international repercussions. As a representative of my government to Washington, I must first insure the secrecy of our operation. That, I am afraid, is the point at issue. As long as the Hardin person lives, our secrecy is breached."

Don Pietro was on his feet, more comfortable now that he could pace back and forth. "Where we been going wrong," he began, sensing-rather than seeing—

the others giving rapt attention, “is that one guy can hide almost anywhere. Particularly in a city this size. We know he likes the desert. So the place to find him is on that damned desert. The trouble with my boys was that they all looked like what they are—to anyone even a little in the know. What we gotta do is make them look like they belong on that stinkin’ desert and take time for a long search.”

“Granted,” His Lordship said softly.

“You know what I mean? Use them dune buggies and jeeps, things like that. Takin’ a crew wagon out there is dumb. The guys that got caught out there can tell you that. So we get the guys tricked up like some bunch of desert nuts. Camping gear, all of that.”

“You have looked into this in detail?” Chau la inquired.

“You bet I did. It’s bothered me from the first. How one guy could pin us down so easy. In here, he’s one face in seven million. Out on that desert, he’s one guy among a bunch of rocks. Give me enough guys and we’re bound to find him. Given a week’s time we’ll eliminate the problem entirely.”

“In the meanwhile, shipments will be stopped until security is obtained.” The Chinese’s voice was final.

“Speakin’ of security,” Don Pietro suddenly added, “what about this Senator? He could mess up the works pretty good.”

After a brief pause, His Lordship replied in an offhand manner. “As I assured you before, we are not to worry about such matters. Our arrangement is protected all the way to the top. I can assure you that Senator Corvus will not go off on an investigation involving us. I am quite sure he will devote his efforts to locating the elusive Mister Hardin."

Mark Hardin was emerging from the sweat lodge when Willard Haskins returned from another information gathering trip to Los Angeles. He greeted the older man, dressed quickly after a brief swim and joined him upstairs.

"Did you know that Senator Corvus was a Rhodes Scholar?"

"Not really. We didn't follow politics much in 'Nam," Mark's reply came, wry with double meaning.

"He was. Spent six years in England. He's more of a lawman than a lawyer. Did a special paper on a comparative study of Scotland Yard procedures and American police methods. It seems we have obtained a most formidable adversary."

"Formidable or not, he's still one of the sheep. I can't go around shooting down the white hats along with the bad guys. How's that squirt gun of yours coming?"

"Excellent. I'm more confident of the dosages now. Given a bit more time, I feel this could become the weapon of the future. Think of the effect it would have on law enforcement."

"Good. What else did you learn about the Senator?"

"He arrived in Los, Angeles two nights ago, is staying at the Beverly Wilshire Hotel and he held a press conference this morning. He said his investigators had sufficient information to begin hearings by midweek."

"That much we know from TV," Mark replied. "Except for his room number. What about a little meat?"

Unruffled, Willard Haskins replied, "Suite eleven-oh-three. Overlooks the lights out toward Century City Plaza. By the way, his Midwestern twang is assumed. He only lived the minimum time necessary in the state that elected him to the Senate. He's from Connecticut."

"Well, well. A bit of an actor," Mark was amused.

"For the best political reasons, my boy, the very best. Corn farmers like to elect other corn farmers to represent them. All the same, I feel we should pay very close attention to the good Senator. A man with his degree of intelligence and imagination could represent a real danger to us."

"Not as real as Don Pietro Scarelli. The Senator will fight with warrants. Scarelli's boys use real bullets."

"Oh, yes, just something in passing. Senator Corvus has a young daughter. Girl went completely hippie. Demonstrations, peace marches, the whole gamut. They haven't spoken in two years. The girl is supposed to be living in a commune in—of all unlikely places—Skagit County, Washington. It seems her father didn't feather out in his dovelike posture until entirely too late for her liking. She moved out, wearing overalls and bare feet. End of childhood."

"Or the beginning of a permanent one," Mark replied with pointed meaning. "Any signs of the Senator's men sniffing around my cover identity or around you?"

"None so far. If the man wasn't so highly considered and well trained in law enforcement, I'd say the whole project was only to grab political advantage."

"May I say a bit in this conversation?" David Red Eagle asked as he entered the room. "Perhaps it is a racial thing with me, but I have grown to distrust any politician from Washington. The more they talk of fairness, law and order, the more they seem to grab. If all the broken treaties mean anything, I would predict that this Senator Corvus will represent a far greater danger to us than all the guns the Mafia can bring to bear."

13

DESERT CAMPAIGN

They came bounding over the desert in jeeps, dune buggies, four-wheel-drive trucks, vans and wagons; a horde of sun worshipers who liked theirs hot, with a touch of sand, please. Every weekend, antlike, these latter-day desert rats poured out of the cities along the coast, in an attempt to get away from smog and crowds—only to create their own smog and crowds. This weekend, there was a difference, a startling, grim difference.

Mingled among the others, they still stuck out; the grim-faced, pinched-featured men with ferret eyes, uncomfortable in their stiff new jeans, shirts and boots, unaccustomed garb for these suited city dwellers. In their buggies, rolligons, jeeps and camping gear they stood apart from the usual habitude of the desert. It was as if Rommel's Afrika Korps had been decked out in civvies and sent to fight yet another desert campaign. The others sensed the differentness about these newcomers, their alienness, but they generally went unremarked about their business.

Unremarked except for the careful scrutiny of Mark Hardin, Professor Willard Haskins and David Red Eagle. The presence of these multi-clad hoods did not ease their minds regarding Mafia retaliation for Mark's one-man holocaust. Surely, the trio had reasoned, following one reeling blow upon another, Don Pietro's men would not launch a search of this magnitude, yet here they were. David Red Eagle had spotted the first ones early that morning, over at the general store in Walter Knott's "Calico Ghost Town."

Three hoods, looking uncomfortable in the heat and their stiff, new "casual" clothes, had entered and bought a six-pack of cokes—the strongest drink allowed by the creator of Knott's Berry Farm, now operator of the old mining town tourist attraction. They had cast their eyes nervously around the room, catching the attention of Red Eagle.

"Hey, Lefty, we was supposed to look for an Indian, right?"

"Right. But the other guy's more important. Why?"

"That's an Indian, right?"

The third hood looked at David Red Eagle. "He's right, Lefty. Hey, Injin!"

"Mande? No soy Indio, soy Mexicano. ¿Que queres, señores?" David replied, faking an excellent Mexican accent.

"Forget it," Lefty snapped to his companions. "He

says he's no Indian, he's a Mex. Screw ya, Mex!" he shouted to Red Eagle as the three departed.

David quickly made his purchases and left for The Stronghold, where they now discussed alternative plans to meet this new threat. Regardless of considerable protest from Mark, Professor Haskins' sensible plan won out.

"It's settled. I insist you see the reasoning. These men are looking for both of you—never mind that David temporarily managed to bluff three of them—and they have a good idea what you look like. We all admit it is time to rid ourselves of the Ferrari. Fine. I'll do it. Take it out on the desert, abandon it and walk back. It's not the first time I've walked this desert alone. I'll take along enough things to provide me a cover—eccentric old desert rat looking for rocks. Let me tend to that. At least, having the car out of the way and having the enemy finding it in the wrong place should tend to confuse them. I know several places that would serve, sites of old mines, such like, that will keep them away from here...provided they have the car as bait."

"At least let me provide a little surprise for them in the car," Mark argued with less persuasiveness than before.

"I'll agree to that. Just make it loud enough to give me some idea how far behind me they are when they locate the car."

"It will be loud enough."

"Good. Can we be ready in half an hour?"

"Definitely," Mark decided. "I'll plan to leave then."

Three hours later, and fifteen miles distant, Professor Haskins suddenly and unexpectedly became a prisoner of the very men he sought to deceive. It was not a capture such as his friends had expected, rather it was a matter of an unlucky choice of paths back to The Stronghold.

Willard Haskins had eluded all pursuit in the speedy foreign car and he had abandoned it near an old mine entrance. Some fifteen minutes and one and a half miles separated him from the car when it was located by the Mafia searchers. He knew exactly when they located it. There was a billowing cloud of dust and smoke, a muffled thump and a slow ground swell.

The pressure-release detonator had mashed into the driver's side door of the Ferrari to set off six pounds of C-4 plastique explosive, eliminating the car and those around it. Smiling with smug satisfaction, Professor Haskins proceeded to his home.

Over another ridge, he stumbled into what was becoming the main base camp for the search parties. Literally stumbling on loose rock, he fell into the arms of three surprised button men from the Las Vegas contingent. They took him down to where Tug Boat Donnelson had set up his command post. With clever, knowing eyes, the Vegas Capo examined his prisoner. His eyes, however, were not clever enough to see through the outward appearance affected by Professor Haskins.

"Who are you?"

Professor Haskins looked up at the men around

him, screwing his face into a semblance of a typical desert rat. "What's it to you, sonny?" he snapped back.

This reply earned him a vicious backhand swipe from one of the hard men who held him before their boss. "Answer the questions," the hard guy snarled.

"One more time, old man. Who are you and what are you doing snoopin' around our camp?"

The professor licked at a small rivulet of blood that formed on his split lip. "I waren't snoopin', mister. I...I always tramp through these hills, on my way over to the highway."

"On your way from where?" Donnelson demanded.

"That's none o'yer business!" Willard Haskins snapped.

"I'm making it my business," the Capo growled. He reached out and bunched up the front of Professor Haskins' shirt, jerking the smaller man toward him. "You answer or we'll make mush outta you. Where from?"

"No use. I got my rights and I got my own place.

I prospect these hills and this desert nigh onto fifty years..."

Another slap brought tears to the old man's eyes. "Gawddamn you! Answer my questions!" Tug Boat and his two goons proceeded to pound Professor Haskins into insensibility.

By three-thirty that afternoon, Mark had become very worried about the professor. Knowing the desert as he did, his prolonged absence was alarming. Had he run afoul of the roving bands of button men looking for

Mark and Red Eagle? Mark paced the floor glancing from time to time out the big picture window.

At three forty-five, he decided to discover the cause of the professor's tardiness. Dressing in light khaki shirt and trousers and pliable desert boots, he made a passable alteration of his features and set out in a jeep to scour the territory, nestled under his tan jacket was his reliable .45 Colt Commander.

Two hours later, with nearly three hours of daylight remaining, he was back, his worst fears a reality. From over one ridge, he had observed that Willard Haskins was a prisoner at the Mafia base camp. Mark's brow furrowed deeply with worry. How could he get the old man out? If he made a direct assault it would tip them to the professor's connection with Mark and he would be dead before a rescue was effected. If he waited, there was a chance they would tire of their present methods of questioning and make a turkey out of him.

Mark had heard of Mafia turkeys before. It wasn't a pleasant thing. Often the victim wound up skinned alive, or tortured to death with a blowtorch or fed to the fish, a piece at a time. He could not wait helplessly and allow this to happen to the kindly patron who had done so much for him. He would have to act, but how?

As he climbed from the jeep, in the cool underground garage, he recalled the professor's latest project; the dart pistol. Granted it wasn't foolproof yet, but even a killing dose—administered silently—just might allow him to enter and leave the camp safely and undiscovered.

His penetration would have to wait for darkness, this he already knew. Quickly he went to the lab and selected several varieties of darts, spare gas cylinders and the pistol.

In his own quarters, he removed the light clothes he had worn, replacing them with crisp, new dark clothing for night work. The men he was going against all wore stiff new clothes, he would adopt the same to ease his penetration. He discarded the .45 for his High Standards. Carefully he affixed the silencers to carbine and pistol alike, made sure he had adequate ammunition and then went to the kitchen for a hasty but light meal.

Darkness was just settling over the lower cuts and arroyos as Mark eased himself into position atop the rise separating him from the Mafia camp. Quickly his eyes scanned the area, locating the sentries—there were only a few and they were widely separated and down close to camp. He nodded satisfaction and slid back over the rim, closing his eyes, waiting for the proper time.

14

NIGHT PROBLEM

At midnight, Mark awoke to his internal alarm clock. Once again he topped the rise. IBs night vision was fully functional and he quickly, located the six sentries. Satisfied that their positions had changed only a little since his sundown observation, Mark began a slow, silent descent toward the camp.

Crouched, hands feeling ahead for any betraying cactus or sagebrush, Mark worked to within a hundred yards of the two sentries on his side of the camp. He eased himself into a comfortable kneeling position, sighted on the red glow of a cigarette tip and squeezed off a round. The silenced Ruger .22 chuffed once, twice, three times. There was a distant, slap of bullet against flesh, a grunt and one sentry was out of the way. Off to his left, he heard a muffled cry.

"What the hell?"

Mark winced. He was aware that anyone along the

trajectory of the bullet would hear the crack as it broke the sound barrier. That was the trouble with a twenty-two. Easy to silence the gun itself, but nothing to be done about the crack of the bullet. For that reason, he was reluctant to Use the carbine, yet distance was necessary to assure a safe corridor out when he had the professor.

Mark whirled into the sound and snapped off two more shots. One smacked home, a startled gasp followed, choked off by the third bullet that also found home. He waited in tense silence to see if anyone responded to the sentry's outcry. A minute passed, two, three. No alarm was raised.

Cautiously, Mark continued into the area. He slung the short carbine over his shoulder and drew his silenced pistol. From the waistband of his trousers he also pulled the plastic dart pistol, clutching it in his left hand. He crossed the remaining space to the camp in short, quiet rushes.

The old thrill he had felt during penetration missions in 'Nam was upon him again. His heart pounded and a giddy sense of excitement coursed through his veins. But he was too much a pro to let it overbalance his caution and determination. This one would have to go off without a hitch. There was no backup this time—no squad or platoon behind him, and no radio to call for air or artillery. He was on his own and on one of the most important penetration missions of his life. There was no either/or about this one. No "bring him out or snuff him." It was bring him out alive or die right there...And the guy who had given those orders was the guy who had to carry them out. Taking a deep breath, Mark advanced around the corner of a low tent....

Bear Brollini had been put in charge of the night guard. He sat beside the fire, drinking coffee for a while until he discovered that it blinded him, and he was unable to see beyond his hand in the outer darkness to check the guards. For better than an hour he sat in his darkened tent, letting his eyes grow accustomed to the Stygian blackness. Once he thought he heard a startled shout in the distance—cut off in the middle—and roused himself, at first thinking he was hearing things. In the silence that followed, he debated whether he had heard anything at all. He decided it was time to check the guards if nothing else. He emerged from the tent. As he straightened up, a dark figure came around the side of the tent.

"Who's that?" he demanded.

The dark figure turned toward him, right hand lifting. "Who'er you?" came a gruff voice from the darkness.

"Brollini, you idiot. Don't go around like that. Trigger happy as some of these guys are, they're liable to burn ya without askin'."

"Bear Brollini?" asked the dark figure, as if he had not heard the rest of the triggerman's conversation.

"Sure, Who else?" It was the last question Bear Brollini asked that night.

Mark was unprepared for the sudden emergence of

a figure from the tent he had crouched beside. Recovering, he brought up his right hand, the silencer-tipped muzzle pointed unwaveringly at the huge man's heart. During their brief conversation, it dawned on him that this was the tenderhearted hood who had always treated his punch drunk informant, Lumpy Louie, with kindness and patience. He switched weapons in midsentence and gently squeezed the trigger. The dart pistol hissed and Bear Brollini slapped at the sting. His slaps ended in a grunt and uncoordinated twitching as he fell to the injection of M-99 and pentothal. He would sleep for more than three hours. Mark moved on, silent as a ghost.

Twice more, Mark encountered restless hoods, prowling the camp at this late hour. Each time he used the High Standard, snuffing out their lives with little concern, dragging them into-absolute darkness between campers and tents. Professor Haskins was not in the tent where Mark had located him that afternoon. A momentary vision of the old man, lifeless eyes turned upward at the desert sky, flashed Over Mark, then he grimly went on with his search.

He found the professor being questioned again in Tug Boat Donnelson's tent. Cautiously working his way to the rear, Mark pulled out his Buck knife and silently slit open the back wall. Voices and the sound of blows covered the sudden ripping of cloth. The razor sharp blade made quick work of the canvas and Mark found himself looking at the scene within. His hackles rose as he took in the condition of his old friend. Bruised and bleeding, he was seated, tied to a director's chair, faced by four mobsters. One of them was lighting a blowtorch. He was the first to fall. Mark had no opportunity to plan it, he simply fired with the dart pistol until it was empty.

All four men lay on the floor of the tent, dead. The four darts Mark had loaded, following the knockout round, were filled with curarine, far more swift and deadly than the curare from which it was extracted. Quickly Mark stepped through the tent and crossed to his friend. He cut the nylon cords that bound Professor Haskins to the chair. Neither man spoke; each realized the hazards of their current situation.

As Willard Haskins rubbed feeling back into his hands and feet, Mark recharged the dart pistol and then glanced around the room. He took a piece of paper from a briefcase on Donnelson's bunk and hastily scrawled a message: "This fight is between Don Pietro and me. Next time you attack an innocent person, everyone will die. Tell the Don I will deal only with him. Send any more punks and they get wasted."

Leaving the way he had entered, Mark brought along a stiff and sore Willard Haskins. He stopped beside the drugged form of Bear Brollini long enough to pin a second note to the man's shirt. It read; "You are alive because you treated Lumpy Louie with kindness. If you are smart, you will be in another state by sunrise." He also picked up the tiny capture dart with which he had downed the gunsel. He had done the same in the tent at the whispered insistence of Professor Haskins. Keep them guessing, off guard, was the name of the game. Even though the four shots fired into the tent were fatal ones, the method of delivery would remain their secret a little longer.

Weapons holstered, the professor shuffling on ahead, they made their way out of camp. At the base of the slope, a figure suddenly rose from the ground, barring their way. "Hold it right there."

Professor Haskins stopped in his tracks, slowly raising his hands away from his sides and upward. The alert street soldier moved across the open space between them, stumbling on the unaccustomed rough ground, but never pointing the muzzle of his revolver away from the center of the old man's chest.

"I don't know how you got away from the boss, you old fart, but you're going back now," growled the hard man. He came closer and reached out to turn the reluctant prisoner. As he did, a thin strand of piano wire descended in a loop over his head. His reactions were no match for the swift death that claimed him.

Mark snapped his crossed wrists back across his body and gave the wire a single, efficient twist, locking it in place. The hood died quickly, his head nearly severed from his body by the garrote. Mark eased him to the ground and motioned to Professor Haskins to follow him.

Once the other side of the ridge, a short mile's hike

brought them to the jeep and they sped for home. Mark was satisfied. The whole operation had taken twelve minutes. Nine dead, six unconscious and the professor freed. A good night's work. But more trouble waited only with the coming of day...

15
A.P.B.

Every morning newscast carried the same announcement. "Following a late night raid, in which nine men lost their lives and two more remain on the critical list at Queen of Angels Hospital, the Los Angeles County Sheriff's Office has issued an All-Points Bulletin for Mark Allen Hardin. He is wanted for murder, assault with a deadly weapon, bombing charges and numerous lesser infractions. The picture you see is the most recent, taken in Saigon when Hardin was a member of the United States Army. He is considered armed and extremely dangerous. Anyone who recognizes the wanted man is urged by authorities to call the local police, the Sheriff's Office or the F.B.I.

"Early this morning, after intensive investigation, a spokesman for Senator Martin Corvus's Subcommittee on Crime and Violence announced that a confidential source within the ranks of organized crime had given them the name of the perpetrator of the wave of violence that has plagued the Southland for the past month and a half. The A.P.B. was issued immediately by the Sheriff's Department and a massive manhunt was launched. We will have more on the search for Mark Hardin following this..."

Mark snipped off the TV and returned to his eggs. He ate with little appetite. The fact that his name was now known to police and criminals alike made life and future movements nearly impossible. If only there was some way to divert this entire thing, let it cool off and later leave the area permanently...But that was wishful thinking.

"It's just wishful thinking," Kelly Patterson said as he slammed down his coffee cup. "We have an entire desert to cover, all of Los Angeles County and who knows what else. That damned headline-hunting politician leaking it to the press before calling us sure botched the job."

"Now, now," placated Dan Griggs. "I told you the Senator was not unconscious of the power of headlines. But he did pass it along to you, right?"

"A lot of good that'll do. We'll get a million reports from a million different places from helpful citizens absolutely positive they just sold our fugitive a cup of coffee. By now this Hardin guy is probably on a friggin' plane to Rio or Argentina."

"Regardless," interjected Shaun Thomas, "I want to go along to this big roundup, Kelly. I just don't believe the guy's through and I want to be in on it when he busts loose again."

"You know I can't let you come along. I can't keep you out of the area, but no riding in official cars."

"Damn it! What's a friend for if not to give a hand? Hell, Kelly, this is Pulitzer Prize material. Just give me one little break, a scoop over the others..."

"Forget it, Shaun. After the fine job that Corvus did, if the Lieutenant even catches us smiling at a member of the press, we'll take our family jewels home in a paper sack. I'll tell you this, though," he relented. "We were assigned the sector around Barstow and as far northeast as the Calico Mountains. If you just happen to be out that way and in a position to observe...well, I can't do anything to stop you."

Shaun Thomas grabbed his notebook and tape recorder and galloped out of Kelly's office. His "Thanks" wafted behind him on the hot summer air.

Bouncing and jolting over the rough ground in a San Bernardino County Sheriff's Department jeep, Kelly envied his reporter friend the air-conditioned comfort of the Oasis Motel cocktail lounge. There, with a secreted police-frequency radio receiver, Shaun was as aware of everything that was happening as Kelly, and he was a hell of a lot more comfortable. Selecting the jeep as a mobile command post had placed the Detective Sergeant at a distinct disadvantage with regard to the weather. His thoughts about the last briefing, given personally by Senator Corvus, did nothing to ease his condition.

"Remember, we must suppose that elements of organized crime are also continuing to search the desert for Hardin," the Senator cautioned. "The last thing we want to see is a cops and robbers shoot-out. The eyes of the entire nation are on this thing and your conduct...your exercise of restraint...is all important. My committee is geared to deal with the criminal element, while you are better suited to find Mark Hardin. With this maniac, gentlemen, I would urge you—off the record of course—to shoot to kill. The man is dangerous...to everyone, as long as he lives. Now, good luck and good hunting."

The whole speech rankled Kelly. Hell, he reasoned, if the guy had stuck to a few hits, avoided these mass slaughters, he'd be a hero. In the back of his mind was the nagging worry about how much the super pure heroin figured in the actions of this Mark Hardin—and that itself was a surprise, listing as their suspect a man that his department had thought was dead. He was half convinced that they were chasing the wrong guy, that their time would be better spent looking into this new supply of poison, its source and channels of distribution. First it was the State Department saying to soft-peddle the Red Chinese connection and hounding after the hit man, then a United States Senator says the most important thing is to get the guy who is cutting up; the ranks of the Mafia. It made a guy wonder....

With a bone-jarring lurch, the jeep slammed to a stop overlooking a long, color-rich valley. Kelly gathered himself and, half crouching, looked down it toward the distant highway. He wiped sweat from his brow, then hefted his binoculars. Painted desert scenery leapt into clear detail as the coated lenses cut through the shimmering heat distortion. Rocky, barren and cactus-strewn, a playground out of hell spread before him. Kelly scanned it in slow, experienced sweeps. Not even the sidewinders were out on a day like this. He grunted and motioned the driver to turn around.

"That all you gonna look at?" asked the San Bernardino sheriff's man.

"For now. My bet is we have more luck at night. We have the men for it, spread out in overlapping box formations, night glasses, snooper scopes and the works. Yeah, night's the time we'll find him."

"What makes you so sure?"

"Hell, man, ask yourself. Would you be out in this...a day like this...if you had good sense and any choice?"

A look of concentration changed to a broad grin on the rookie deputy's face. "Yeah. Tonight's the night..."

16

DEAD END

Three nights later, restlessness from his enforced inactivity got the best of Mark Hardin. He had fumed at the inept manner the press, in conjunction with Senator Corvus, had handled the entire situation. They had made him a monster, bent on taking lives indiscriminately. All the bleeding hearts and the antigun nuts had jumped on the bandwagon and were decrying him as a "mad dog killer," slaughtering the helpless innocent. No mention was made that the men who died were hardened criminals, that it had all started out as a penetration of a huge new drug smuggling and distribution ring. In fact, the remarkably pure drugs he had left behind at this first strike had been completely forgotten in the heat of all that had gone after. Frustration was pushing Mark to recklessness.

If only, he thought, he could slip out in darkness. There was no moon that night and it was perfect for a hit. Get the street soldiers to shoot at each other and maybe the law would move in, using that as an excuse to round up a lot of hoods. Anyway, it was worth a try.

At ten-thirty that night, Mark—dressed entirely in soft, midnight-blue clothes—slipped from The Stronghold and blended into the night's blackness.

Mark had to cover some three miles until he came to the site of gangland activity. He moved with fluid ease, the High Standard riding comfortably on his right hip, the dart pistol—which he had come to like very much during the liberation of Willard Haskins—snug in a shoulder holster. With catlike pounces, silent in his soft moccasins, Mark moved within hearing distance of two groups, listening until he had several names from each. Then he faded to one side and stealthily approached the head of one party.

"Hey, Carmine. I heard something over there," Mark whispered softly into the ear of the button man leading group number one. The guy was good, he didn't start at the sudden, disembodied voice.

"Yeah, where?"

"C'mon, bring the others. Molto silencio, capisce?" Mark clinched it with his command of Italian. The six-man hunting party moved off behind him. He led them a short distance, then halted them about twenty yards from the front of the other party. Silently, he faded away.

"Manny? Gimp?" The voice from the darkness whispering urgently to them knew their names, so it must be one of theirs, right?

"Yeah. What is it?" the leader of group number two asked in an equally soft whisper.

"Nobody move. There's a guy out there. Right in front of us."

"Yeah? Where?" The first uneasy hint of suspicion. "I don't see nuttin'."

"Look, ya dummy. Right over there. Walk real soft about five paces, you'll damn near fall over him."

"Mother of God! Ya mean we got this Hardin prick?"

Changing his position slightly, Mark Hardin unsnapped the silencer from his .22 autoloader. "You sure have!" he shouted, diving to one side as he fired three fast shots into Manny's startled face. As their leader fell dead, the others returned fire.

"He's out there!" Gimpy shouted.

Their bullets tore into the unsuspecting bodies of the first group. Taken by surprise, they returned fire. Soon more guns joined, in, shouts were raised and more men joined the battle. Mark Hardin started to slip away. Then came the unexpected. A spotlight lanced out of darkness, pinning him against the night like a bug on a laboratory slide. Mark's reflexes saved his life as he leaped aside, back into darkness, before bullets whistled through the space he had just occupied.

He broke into a loose-jointed run, dodging boulders and cactus as he tried desperately to escape the closing dragnet. Suddenly, from his left, other lights cut into the night.

"This is the Sheriff's Department. Throw down your

guns. You are shooting each other and at our men. Throw down your guns. Mark Hardin! Hardin, if you are out there, surrender at once. Resistance is futile. Give yourself up! You are surrounded and cut off from any escape. Do not shoot!"

Pumping his legs, twisting and turning from one cut in the ground to another, Mark tried to outdistance pursuit. He left the lights and bullhorn in his wake, but behind him, he could still hear the pounding of many feet, as police and hoods alike hounded his trail. His breath was ragged and he exerted every last ounce of energy in his attempt to evade capture. No matter which side got him, he was sure, it meant death before the sun came up.

Just as the sound of his hunters began to diminish behind—as undisciplined, poorly conditioned bodies tired and slowed down—Mark made a fatal mistake. He turned into a wide arroyo that narrowed and deepened, only to end in a sheer cliff face. He was trapped in a box canyon! Stifling his own gasping breath, he heard the pursuers enter behind him and begin to close in. Desperately, he looked around, seeking any available cover, determined to make a last stand. Nothing offered itself as a barricade. He was trapped in the open. There was nothing for it now but to climb. Climb and hope that there was a way to the top.

The first sixty feet up were simple, broken and slanted, but easy to climb with little effort. From below, Mark heard the voices of several men as they came to the dead end. Striving for quiet, praying that his movements would not betray him, he began the next phase of his ascent.

Now the surface changed to nearly vertical sandstone. Mark clung with toe-hold purchases as his hands explored above him, finding another pocket and painfully, slowly dragging his body along, ever upward. He made thirty feet, forty. He stopped to rest. Blood was pounding in his ears, dimming the sounds of activity below. More button men had entered the canyon, he knew, but he was unsure of the identity of the first arrivals until an amplified voice reached him.

"Police officers, drop your weapons."

There were police below him as well as hoods on who knew how many sides. Smothering a groan, forcing his muscles, Mark inched upward again. His hand grasped something cold, scaly. Instinctively he flung the heavy bodied rattler from him: away and down. It hit with a clatter of stones and an angry buzzing. Flashlights bit through the darkness from below and from the opposite side. They found the snake and, after a few moments, winked out again. Mark inched onward.

Slowly, he became aware of a numbness in the small of his back, first warning of his body failing him as it had done before. If his back gave out now, he was done for. Sore muscles and aching shoulder joints protested, as he strained up another few feet. His toes caught, let go and caught again. Already he could feel a loss of control as the nerves in the small of his back stopped transmitting impulses because of the increasing pressure from the compressed discs: A cold sweat of fear broke out on his face. If his old injury betrayed, him now, if his back let him down this time, there would be ho forty-yard field goal in the final seconds to win the game. Just a short fall in a long darkness and a long time dead.

Agonizingly, he reached out and pulled again. Not far to go, he was sure. Already, by throwing back his head all the way, he could discern a lightening of the blackness before him. Yet he was as helpless as any man could get in his position. All feeling had left his legs and only the power of his superbly conditioned shoulders and arms was left to drag him on. Biting his lip to stifle any sound, he reached out again, with one arm pulling, the other holding him in place. Only inches at a time could be covered now and time was running out. He reached up again and found...nothing!

With a final, agonizing heave, Mark threw himself over the top of the canyon wall and fell face-first into the sandy soil. He was defeated, he knew it. Without legs to carry him, how could he get away from the area where now the search concentrated? Panting, half-blinded by overexertion and desperation, he bent to massage his numb limbs. A violent twinge of pain flattened him again. He lay, panting.

Mark felt more than heard the stealthy approach of someone very woods-wise. The unseen person moved with very little sound across the crunchy gravel and sand of the mesa top. Hope flared. David Red Eagle had come looking for him and had guessed his route of escape. He could make it yet. Hope flared and died rapidly as the figure moved-into view.

It was not the soft moccasined feet of his friend and healer. Lifting his head to look up at the approaching man, Mark saw a pair of roughout desert boots. Above them a pair of khaki trouser cuffs. He was stunned. He had never suspected any of the Mafia crewmen would be able to walk so quietly, exhibit such knowledge of silent stalking. But that was all in the history books now. A burning fury took over Mark's mind. If he was going to get it, at least he'd get it taking out a few more of them. His hand clawed for the dart pistol and he pushed himself away from the ground. He'd show them how to die.

"Hokka he!" he shouted in his mind. "It's a good day to die!"

Mark came face to face with the man he believed to be his killer...his gun faltered, the muzzle lowered. An-open, freckled Irish face like that before him could never belong to a Mafia street soldier. Stalemate held them as the other likewise lowered his service revolver. .

"You're one damn hard man to find, Mark Hardin," the man said softly. "You're wanted for a lot of killings. I'm Sergeant Kelly Patterson, Los Angeles Sheriff's Department."

Mark laid down his dart pistol, slowly pushing himself upright. "That tears it, then. I'm through. Just as well the law as the Mafia," Mark said in disgusted resignation. .

17

TRUCE

Suddenly Kelly extended a hand, helping Mark, into a sitting position. Observing his prisoner's helplessness, Kelly had returned his service revolver to its belt holster; he moved quickly to assist the other man. His whispered voice indicated his desire to keep their presence secret.

"You know, Hardin, we're all alone up here. My nearest unit is about a half a mile away and there's nothing but hoods and assorted other types down in that canyon. To top it off, I haven't a walkie-talkie with me."

Mark sat still, studying the man who had done what none of the others could do. His captor was a youthful-looking, open-faced guy who Mark judged to be about ten years his senior.

"What's it going to be?" he asked finally. "I know what we did in 'Nam when there wasn't adequate prisoner security. You going to bring me in over your saddle, so to speak?"

"Cut the crap, Hardin. Let's... let's call it a truce—an armed truce more or less. You have a gun and so do I. Mine makes a little more noise than yours and I'll lay odds you don't want much noise right now. And I'll also lay odds you won't burn down a cop." Kelly Patterson paused a second, gathering his thoughts. "Funny, but I just can't seem to get excited about being the one to bring you in. We're surrounded by Mafia types and trigger-itchy reserve deputies and all I can think of is getting out of here with a whole skin. You willing to cooperate that far?"

A slow grin spread over Mark's face. His head was clearing and the exhausting effects of his climb were lessening. Now he recognized the name of his captor. It was the sheriff's detective labeled by Professor Haskins as one at least neutral about Mark's exploits. "At least that far," he replied.

"You are a wise man, Sergeant," David Red Eagle's voice came softly from the darkness. As he came closer, the other two saw the bow he carried, an arrow notched and ready. "I could have dropped you before you had a chance to draw. Now, it seems unnecessary."

"Hell." Kelly blurted. "Looks like I outfoxed myself."

"You are good, very good," the old Indian responded with honesty. "I had a hard time hearing you myself." Mark knew this to be a stretching of the truth but he held his tongue. "Much too good, I believe, to ever be taken in by the things said in the press." His black eyes bored into Kelly's. "You have been in this from the start, am I right?"

"That you are."

"And you have no curiosity about the heroin Mark left behind?"

"Sure I do. In fact, I feel it is more important than this..." he left off suddenly, realizing he had told two men who were supposed to be enemies far too much.

"As I thought. You are a good policeman. A good one and an honest one. Let's leave here. There is much we should discuss." Mark was surprised and amused. He had never heard David at his diplomatic best and he was enjoying the experience.

Kelly looked from Red Eagle to the silent Mark Hardin. He shrugged his shoulders. "I'm outmanned and outgunned. Do I have any choice?"

An hour later, Mark Hardin, his penetration team and Kelly Patterson were seated in The Stronghold, drinks in hand. The last few miles, Kelly had been blindfolded, but a sudden widening of his eyes told the others that his orientation on the desert was excellent and that he recognized their whereabouts.

He took a deep pull on his drink and lighted a cigarette.

"Quite a layout you have here, sir," he addressed himself to Professor Haskins. "I came—more or less—under duress. What is the point of it all? You could have done me in on the top of that mesa. Why not?"

"It would help greatly, Sergeant," Willard Haskins

mediated, "if you would overcome the innate hostilities you doubtless feel toward anyone who has been declared outside the law. We have what we believe to be just reasons for doing as we do."

"Don't let Professor Haskins overstep himself," Mark added. "He merely provides intelligence and a base camp."

"Not so, my boy. Remember the Ferrari?"

Kelly snorted. "When you guys are through being noble and self-sacrificing, let's get down to it. You have a reason for me being here. What is it?"

"Granted." Mark paused to take another swallow of his Irish whiskey. "Out there you said that the heroin had been on your mind all the while. You even went so far as to say you thought tracing it was more important than finding me. Why?"

"Let's face it. You left us a big fat clue but no picture to fit it into. As a detective—and a good one, I think—I was puzzled and intrigued by the heroin and why it was left behind. Then all hell started to bust loose. The whole basis of the, investigation shifted from trying to find out about the heroin to finding out about you.

"As long as we are laying all of our cards on the table, let me ask you a few questions. First, did you know that the Chinese you shot was connected to the Red Chinese Mission to the UN? Next, did you know his name? And lastly, do you have any idea of the distribution route?"

"No, to all three. I'm not surprised he was from mainland China. My information sources mentioned

Orientals. Another one we know of—do you?—is a character the mob calls His Lordship. Seems to be some sort of wheel in the operation."

"That's a new one on me. You have any lines on him?"

Mark grew thoughtful, studying the detective closely before continuing. "Maybe. First, did you know I knocked over a second shipment of smack?"

"The hell! That's one they would never report. We did have reports of strange lights and gunfire in the City of Commerce one night, but the units arriving on the scene found nothing but some burnt-out flares...That was you?"

"Yep. Before we go on, let me explain a few things. Fill you in on how this whole operation began, because we agree with you, the most important thing is this heroin. We want to find its source, its protection, and then eliminate the entire operation."

For the next half hour, Mark took Kelly over old ground filling him in on his reason for becoming involved. Then he went over recent events—omitting only Lumpy Louie's name and the fact that Bear Brollini had apparently taken advantage of his reprieve and fled the area. When it was all over, the four men drank in silence.

"Now," Mark began, "let's get into this His Lordship thing. One man I have been wondering about for a long time is Senator Corvus. At first I felt he was just a political opportunist, trying to pave the way to the White House with praise from the Law and Order crowd.

Then, as he figured more and more in the adverse things related to my operation, I wondered if he might be a bought man. Maybe through campaign donations that, once accepted, would be too embarrassing to reveal publicly. Then Willard here did some research on the man that made me wonder..."

"Let me interrupt here," Kelly took in their faces before continuing. "I'm pretty close to Dan Griggs, the chief investigator for Corvus. If he's any criteria, the Senator is as pure as driven snow."

"Back in the thirties and forties, they called heroin snow, remember?" Professor Haskins supplied in a droll voice.

"Touché. Just what is it that causes you to suspect Senator Corvus, Mark?" Kelly had slipped into the first name habit some while back. The significance of it was not lost on the three men before him.

"At first it didn't register. Then...well, it was this. According to the inside feelers I have, this guy His Lordship got his moniker from his voice. Veddy veddy uppah-clahss English. So, Martyn Corvus was a Rhodes Scholar. Spent six years in England, best schools, he even did papers on comparative police procedures. Close to a lot of upper-class English accents over a period of time, right? If you pulled my file from the army, you know I spent a number of years in the super cop role. I'll lay odds your first reaction to His Lordship was the same as mine, somebody in a British bank branch, a consulate or embassy. Right?"

"Score one for your side. But why not?"

"That's what took a little longer. I learned from my most reliable contact that Don Pietro was gloating about immunity inside the States. Not across borders, but inside the U.S. Maybe I should be stood in a corner for even suspecting a man like the Senator. Either way, I have a plan for finding out. I sent a ransom note offering to sell back the heroin I took. I'm sending another. In it, I will demand a deal only with the top three men: Don Pietro, His Lordship and, whoever the Chinese send.

"I know it's a lot to ask," Mark went on to another point, "but I do hope you trust me to bring this off and end the heroin supply. If it would help prove my intentions, I'll even let you take the real stuff. I can use a substitute."

"And if you do that, Mark?"

"I'll end up having to snuff them all."

"Then keep it. I may be called a nut for this. I might lose all I have worked for in the department, but I think I like your idea. Let's hear the plan and tell me what you need from me."

"First of all, Kelly, I need time. That only you can provide. Next, I need a small piece of equipment..."

18
YOUR LAST CHANCE

Don Pietro Scarelli was surprised and impressed the first time he met His Lordship face to face. His surprise at the aloof gentleman's identity nearly overshadowed his flaming anger at the second note sent by Mark Hardin. Along with His Lordship and Don Pietro, a third man sat in the study of the big house on Westwood drive. It was Bok Lin Ti, an attaché to the People's Cultural Mission in Washington. His face was impassive as the Mafia Don railed against Mark.

"Last chance, he says. This goddamned punk tells us we have to meet him in person and bring another quarter-million in cash to get back our own heroin! We'll meet. By God, we will meet this bastard."

"It would be foolish to hazard both of us," Lin Ti admonished. "I am sure you agree with that."

"Indubitably, old boy," His Lordship answered.

"If this is a trap, as you suspect, Scarelli, why not

handle the whole matter yourself? Cheat a little on him?"

"Look, both of you. This guy has given us an offer we just can't refuse. We get back the chopper, the fink pilot and our stuff for the money. With all the heat on just now, this will be the last shipment, am I right?"

"We find it to be an untenable position," the Chinese admitted. "As far as we are concerned, the deal is off, as you Westerners say."

"So, at least this way, we have the stuff to keep the chain going until the frogs can start supplying. They're hungry anyway, so why not? Same game as far as we're concerned, right?" His last remark was directed to His Lordship.

"Provided we weather this mess."

"That we can do. I got a plan. He's named the place in the desert where he wants to meet us. Says he'll come by chopper but he wants a pass out. It's just too much to expect, right? So, we set up an ambush a long time before the meet. I got about eighty guys we can use if you think we need that many. Spot them all over the place. We go in, show ourselves—what the hell, he ain't gonna live long enough to tell anyone who we are. We make the deal and then hit him. Mister Wise-ass is all done in. Then it's back to business as usual."

Silence prevailed for several moments. "As I say, we are no longer concerned with this operation. As far as it goes, the plan sounds workable. I would favor it if we were sure of eliminating this man once and for all. So far your men have not performed in a manner that would inspire confidence in future success."

"Rooster ass! This time we know what it is we're up against and we know how to take care of it. All it will amount to is a little drive in the country. What about you?"

His Lordship smiled at the others. "I am inclined to think you are right. After four days and nights of unsuccessful searching, the law has twenty of your men under arrest and nothing else. And they've called off the search. We will have a free hand out there and a chance to set up a good trap of our own. I still have my reservations, but...just maybe, Peter, you have the answer. Never forget that Mr. Bok and I are extremely vulnerable. One slip and the entire thing goes up around us. Now, how do you figure to do it this time, when you've failed so many times before?"

Smarting under their criticisms, Don Pietro went to his desk. He fought down an angry outburst as he unrolled a large contour map of the area and pointed to a hilly section circled in red. "This is the place he named." His voice was smooth, even, not betraying the seething hatred he felt toward these two. "You can see there are plenty of hills around it, a lot of places to hide men and only one road in and out. There's an old mine up there but it is supposed to be flooded and collapsed. No way anyone can surprise us from there if my men are inside before daybreak. Got it so far? Now, we come in two cars. Soldiers in front. We go in my Rolls. We put the guys here, on the road, all around the sides of them hills."

"And we could be annihilated in the crossfire."

"Naw. We do just like he says. Then, when he's on his way out...he can't shoot with an armful of money, right? We let him get part way out, then everyone falls on him. Simple."

The others studied the map for a few moments. The old Don had put in a lot of careful work and it was reflected in the attention to details of the plan laid before them. "Yes," His Lordship thought aloud. "It might work. It could indeed. I'll consent to this scheme on one condition. I want your men to have a rehearsal. Preferably in the exact location. Once they all know precisely what to do, I will rest easier. Can you do that?"

"You bet. Well do it today. Then late tonight they can move into place and we'll have this punk...."

19

VALLEY OF THE SHADOW

"Everyone is in place. We've checked out everything. Even looked for landmines and booby traps. Nothin'. Maybe this bird's gonna play it straight."

"I'll believe that, when I have his head in a paper sack," Don Pietro snapped back over the radio to his man in charge in the canyon. "But you guys did a good job. Ten minutes and we're on our way in. Good hunting."

Time passed at a crawl. At two minutes before the jumpoff, Don Pietro's driver started, the quiet engine of the Rolls Royce and eased off the brake. Ahead of them a carload of gunmen did the same. Time.

Dust blew away from the two cars as they came to a halt in the center of the small canyon floor. So far so good. Not a single breach of discipline among the waiting men. No one socialized, no cigarette smoke gave away a position. Five more minutes. It was all going according to schedule.

Five minutes passed. No helicopter. Five more. Everyone grew restless. Don Pietro sweated. He craned his neck to see the sides of the canyon. Five more minutes passed.

"There's been a little change of plan!" Mark's voice suddenly boomed down from high on the slope. "I'm already on the ground. In exactly five minutes, your chopper will come over. My assistant will lower the goods and you may examine them. If they meet your satisfaction, signal me up here and then send a van uphill toward my voice, carrying the money. Have him walk exactly two hundred paces. Not one more or less. Have him set down the money and turn back. Once he is back at the car, the chopper will land. My man will take the money and come up the rest of the way. Then, as agreed, we will leave without harm.

"Now I want Don Pietro, this fancy English dude and the other top man to get out of the car and show themselves."

Looking at each other, the three men climbed from the Rolls. "I thought you had covered every possible situation," His Lordship whispered, sotto voce.

From above, the voice boomed again. "Now, gentlemen, we will wait."

They heard the chopper before it came into view, a fluttery beating of air, and at last the machine hovered over them. Again, Mark's voice roared. "Is this change agreed to?"

"Well?" queried Bok Lin.

"He must have slipped in before dawn and taken out the boys in that mine. That's where I think he is."

"Where does that leave your plan?" His Lordship wanted to know.

"Don't worry. He ain't leavin' this place. Do we agree?" The others nodded reluctant agreement and Don Pietro waved to the source of the sound.

At once, the helicopter lowered until it was only sixty feet above the ground. A strong downdraft whipped at their clothes, dust billowed outward. From the hovering craft, a canvas bag descended on a long nylon cord. Don Pietro grabbed for it while it was still over their heads; he drew it close and opened it with anxious fingers.

"It's the stuff, all right." he assured the others. They tested it with a small kit produced from Bok Lin Ti's inside coat pocket before agreeing. "Tony," called the Don to his new house manager. "C'mere and take this up the hill."

As they watched, Tony Gallo started up toward the mine entrance above. He carefully counted off two hundred paces and stopped, putting the case on the ground.

"Open it," commanded the electronically assisted voice.

Tony opened it, held it up for inspection and set it down as commanded by the unseen voice. He walked quickly back to the car. Everyone breathed easier.

"Everything according to plan," Don Pietro gloated.

Then everything went very unaccording to plan.

Instead of lowering to a landing, the helicopter began a rapid spiral that took it up in altitude. Don Pietro uttered a strangled oath and jerked his seldom-used .38 from under his coat, blasting off shots at the fleeing vehicle. More fire poured in from the hillsides. Then something was dropping from the passenger side of the chopper. A large, round, odd-shaped, silvery object. It hurtled downward.

His Lordship, Senator Martyn Corvus, recalled later that he stood openmouthed in amazement as the object fell. His last conscious thought was: "By God, it is a beer keg!"

It was indeed a beer keg. But this keg contained some two hundred pounds of sixty-percent nitro dynamite, riding on top of an impact detonator. The blast was tremendous! Men were hurtled through the air to smash against rocks and cactus, others were bowled over on the ground and tumbled to bloody ruin. Shards of the keg formed razor-sharp shrapnel that cut down several hoods, who had exposed themselves to get a better angle of fire at the retreating chopper. Nearly everyone else was knocked unconscious.

Then, from the helicopter, Mark leaned out the door and—using the second thing provided by Kelly—hosed down the area with an M-16 rifle. He confined his shots to the perimeter of the blast area, providing covering fire for David Red Eagle, as he ran down, snatched the money and returned to the mine to collect the tape recorder, amplifier and speaker he had operated from the entrance.

The whirlybird dipped at the top of the rise to take him and his cargo aboard. Then they spun away.

Behind them the low growl of sirens was unheard as a dozen cars of law officers rolled into the area. Waiting for them was a headless Don Pietro Scarelli, a senseless Chinese diplomat and a bleeding, and unconscious United States Senator, Martyn Corvus, his hands still clutching a quarter-million-dollar bag of heroin.

"All in all, it was a pretty good day's work." Mark was feeling well-satisfied as they slipped over the horizon on their way—this time with temporary immunity—back to The Stronghold. His reverie was interrupted by Larry Novak.

"You said you were a pilot. Think you can handle this job?"

"Never flown one before, Larry. Why?"

"Didn't want to slow you down before, but I caught a good one back there. I'm about leaked out now. Nothin' to it. I can get us there, but you gotta land it. Just push forward on this stick to tilt, use the pedals and throttle to bring us down Uh, God, it hurts."

The little pilot was dead when they landed with a solid thump that removed part of the undercarriage and snapped a rotor blade.

End of a mission.

EPILOGUE

LARRY NOVAK'S DEATH BLUNTED THE PLEASURE OF their victory celebration. Yet, it was hard to restrain a shout of joy from Professor Haskins as they heard on the evening news of the arrest of Senator Corvus as head of the drug ring, exposure of his Mafia connections, the resignation of Dan Griggs from the Senator's staff and the expulsion of Bok Lin Ti. The People's Republic of China rescinded the protection of diplomatic immunity for the unfortunate attaché and it was rumored that he was being held for trial in this country.

Don Pietro Scarelli's empire had fallen with the master's death and the members scattered to other spots that harbored their slimy breed: Mark Hardin sat in dark contemplation as the TV was turned off.

"You are troubled about the pilot?" David Red Eagle inquired.

"Not that so much. I suppose we can consider the score settled for Donna now. That and a big one for a lot of kids that have died in the agony/ecstasy of that powdered poison they were peddling. But now what? Where can I go from now on? What can I do?"

"May I suggest something?" Willard Haskins interjected. "You have nearly three-quarters of a million dollars of Syndicate money. You have an excellent cover identity as Jim Hanson that has not been compromised. You yourself admitted, at the outset, that the skills you learned in the army—especially in Vietnam—made you exceptionally well qualified for this undertaking.

"In temperament," Professor Haskins changed tack, "you are ideally suited for the task—or call it a mission if you prefer. You don't enjoy killing, take some sick pleasure in it, but when necessary you kill efficiently.

"You are single, with no family that could let them get a handle on you, as they call it, and force you to surface. You have health, strength and youth. Can you offer any sane reason why you should stop fighting every aspect of this sickness that is killing our nation and its people? Can you offer any reason at all? Could you accomplish anything more by establishing a memorial fund in Donna's name with the money? Would that make you feel any better? Would she rest any better?"

"Get off that, damn it!" Mark snapped. "Look, I'm not Don Quixote chasing windmills. No knight in armor defending fair maidens. I have a normal man's appetites: I lust for women, I like my booze, I get hungry, cold, scared. What's done is done. Why not let it rest there?"

"Why? That's the proper question. Oh, you should

have a rest, you deserve a change for a while. But, my boy, what I am saying is that you have the power to do something really big. Do things no officer of the law could dream of doing. You can bring these scum into the healing light of day."

"How? As a fugitive, a mad bomber?"

"Visitor," interrupted David.

"How far away?" they both accepted his pronouncement.

"Just turned into the road. Two minutes."

It was Kelly Patterson. His Irish face beamed with triumph. "Good news all around, friends," he announced as he entered. "You, my friend, are a very lucky lad. Between Dan's and my own modest efforts, we succeeded in getting all of the charges dropped against you. You're a free man, Mark. Of course, we had to ignore a couple of laws and bend a few others. But, as long as you don't do anything like this again in California, the governor has decided to declare amnesty—to clear you of all charges. He urges your early departure for other places,

"Another thing. I may get a promotion out of this. Seems as how a reporter did a big story about how I masterminded this whole thing and now the Sheriff's faced with the decision of either kicking me upstairs or giving me an unauthorized pay raise.

"Lastly, about the federal things. The ATF boys screamed and frothed at the mouth about the silencers, bombs and other illegal devices, but as a special investigator on his staff, Dan Griggs convinced them you were empowered to use any devices authorized for other federal officers."

"Hell, I'm no federal cop."

"You became one for convenience, whether you knew it or not. It's that or a long stay on McNiel Island. By the way, that job's permanently open—at least now. Dan is going on to a very special, hush-hush job with Justice. He says he likes your style and you can come to work for him and do it legally."

"I never wanted a license to kill and I don't want one now. I set out to get vengeance and I got it. Tell your friend thanks, but no thanks."

"You may wish you had taken him up on it."

"Not me. I'm headed for a little R-and-R, then a new name, a new place and the quiet life for me."

"I don't believe it," Kelly quipped. "But just for openers, where do you figure on taking this R-and-R?"

"Haven't given it much thought," Mark told the detective. "Tahoe, maybe Reno or Vegas. Might even take in some of Mexico. But first there's a little social obligation I have to keep. A girl friend of Donna's. She wanted a personal report on how it all came out. I'm gonna have dinner with her and we'll see from there. We'll see."

BLOOD ON THE STRIP: THE PENETRATOR SERIES BOOK II

Evil brings The Penetrator to Las Vegas. A town given life by corruption and nourished by greed. A town where all that glitters is not gold but perhaps the flash of a knife blade destined for The Penetrators heart. In Las Vegas he seeks an elusive enemy, but for Hardin even one faint clue is enough.

AVAILABLE NOW ON AMAZON

ABOUT THE AUTHOR

Chet Cunningham made his home in San Diego, California, and was a prolific writer of novels and nonfiction. He came from a newspaper background, so he was geared to produce writing every day and not just when "the muse moved [him]." He has been quoted as saying he doesn't believe in writer's block.

In 1950, Cunningham was drafted in the Army. After nine months in Japan, he was sent to the front lines of the war in Korea. He participated in two battles and numerous line-crossings and prisoner patrols. Assigned to a heavy weapons company, he served as an 81 mm mortar gunner, squad leader, and section leader. His service earned him the Combat Infantryman's Badge. Upon conclusion of two years of service, he was discharged in the rank of sergeant.

He graduated from Pacific University in Forest Grove, Oregon with a BA in journalism, and after his hitch in the Army he received his MS degree from the Columbia University Graduated School in Journalism in New York City in 1954.

Chet passed away at age 88 in March 2017.

Printed in Dunstable, United Kingdom

66875199R00112